Smithy & Suzie

I0742636

Also by Ray Clift and published by Ginninderra Press

Fiction

The Journey of Hamlyn Baylis Wells

Always In Denial

Smithy's Cupboard

Shaken & Stirred

Shalom Samuel

The Last Journey of Hamlin Baylis Wells

She Walks the Line

Non-fiction

Maybe Blue Ghosts

It's a Fine Line

Cops, Crooks, Courts & Spooks

Ray Clift

Smithy & Suzie

My everlasting thanks goes to my family:
Ann, who gives me the space, feeds me and is always there;
my daughters Kerry and Jo and their partners for their
continual support; and all our grandchildren.

Smithy & Suzie
ISBN 978 1 74027 962 8
Copyright text © Ray Clift 2015
Cover: Gary MacRae

First published separately as *Smithy's Cupboard* 2011
and *She Walks the Line* 2014

This edition published 2015 by
GINNINDERRA PRESS
PO Box 3461 Port Adelaide SA 5015
www.ginninderrapress.com.au

Contents

Smithy's Cupboard

Prologue

Melbourne, Australia, 2005

Smithy climbed the few stairs, passing by old Ted the black Labrador, deaf and happy with his frequent naps and snores. He straightened his front legs, stretching and wagging his tail slightly, yet would not respond to the urgings of his master to climb the stairs. He sat with his chin resting on his front paws, his eyes were wide open, unblinking and starey with a look of fear on his features.

'You've seen things a dog shouldn't see – haven't you, mate?'

Ted whimpered in reply.

Smithy saw the moonlight with its cascade flittering down the curtains which were hand-made by Joan many years ago. The pleats still hung firm and straight along with the hems all proudly sewn in a time when happiness and adventure held pride of place in their lives.

He looked at Ted before entering the master bedroom. 'I wish you'd met her, Ted.'

The dog groaned in response as if he had picked up the vibration of his master's voice, yet he still refused to look up.

Smithy stood in front of the mirrored robes and gazed at the figure which sent a message to him of long ago when he was an SAS trooper in the Australian Army. The mirror replied without any sound being heard, 'Slack soldier,' and the reflection spoke back, 'I agree.'

The neighbours would have heard the vigorous teeth-brushing ritual with the tap being turned on and off: the ceaseless water hammer replying each time until the ritual was finished. David Alexander Smith hated wasting water. Gargling sounds would have also been heard and clocks would have been set at 1800 hours by the folk next door – signifying the nightly news was about to commence. He wiped his face on the unwashed lavender hue hand towel which was kept inside Joan's glory box and brought out after the wedding in 1969. He gazed at the towel and knew she would have hated his neglect of her treasured gift.

The 1800 news held no interest for Dave. He entered the robes and tossed his clothes on top of the expanding pile of crumpled food-stained articles, discarded , ignored and hovering parallel with the plimsoll line. He squatted in the small space which he had cleared, enabling his slender hindquarters to fit comfortably just like he did when he made hides in South Vietnam. He found a comfort within his space in the wardrobe and he was able to dwell on the musty smells, some having a residue of camphor flakes. Those odours revealed evocative moments of long ago when he was vigorous and buoyant.

His frozen smile remained when he remembered how they jived together and the dance hall clapped

Edward Smith, usually called Ted (Smithy named his dog Ted in honour of the patriarch of the family), would never have gone off the rails like his son. Smithy knew his father had a life which was preordained. It was as if a parchment had fallen from great heights without damage, with a mission inscribed.

The parchment had acquired creases with age, built up red dust from the Mallee farming country. Some microdots of spillage might have faded the parchment rules yet the mission remained intact like an unmovable granite boulder.

Edward walked out each day at the same time and mounted the giant tractor with his two dogs already in the cabin, tails wagging and yelping in excitement. He was armed with sandwiches lovingly made the night before by his wife Maud. Beef and pickles one day, cheese and chutney the next. An apple munched later to clean his teeth and great swigs from his screw-top bottle of black tea, no sugar, no milk. Off they would roam all day over the vast broad acres of wheat, barley and oats She would welcome him home at dusk and the family ate together. Sleep would prevail after he counted the stars blinking through the skylight, shining the bedroom. What wonderful times, he mused

There came a time after Maud died when he missed the years of stability. However, Ted still worked the land with Smithy's brother Adam. Smithy loved to reflect on those times.

He thought about the walking frame they bought for Ted. It slowed his pace and his injuries from his time as an army engineer in World War II did not help. Although it made him appear brittle, the power in the man was obvious. When he spoke anywhere about anything, people stopped and listened, as if Moses had returned with an addendum.

'What would he think of me now?' Dave grimaced, thinking of the enemies he had killed in battle from his hidden spots.

The killing outside of the military caused him some nightmares, however, and he struggled putting the thoughts aside in the way he usually did – in separate folders, as if his mind was a computer.

He rose to his feet and threw a yellowed robe with his initials emblazoned in bold green and walked to the mirror.

'Am I searching for my real self? There's a double marching alongside me. Is it taking over?' And those thoughts flooded his dreams in the cupboard, the lounge and the bed. 'Will I be forgiven?' was a thought which remained in focus during waking hours and in sleep.

1

Smithy

I was born in 1947. The war had ended and the broad-acre family farm in the Wimmera district in the Mallee country of Victoria had returned to a version of normal in the two years after hostilities had concluded, though some rationing had continued.

A handle was delivered to me when I was a baby and it stuck. My Uncle Ron was a blacksmith and a sapper in the Engineers, fighting alongside Edward, my father. Ron spotted my red face and legs and proclaimed in his loud voice (developed above the hammer blows and to counter his slight deafness), 'Gonna be another blacksmith? Another Smithy?'

My older brother Adam was about seven years of age when I was born and my grandparents and he busied themselves with all the chores until Dad marched in the door just before the war ended. Adam was, and still is, a role model of how to be a great older brother, gentle yet tough, and those big hands put many a bully on his back. I guess he and Dad were always my heroes. They taught me how to watch the signs in the sky, the movement of clouds, flocks of birds, ants, and how to fashion metal in our old ramshackle blacksmith shop stuck idly between two sheds years ago, so that the old roof could be joined without further beams. Very economical, versatile and ingenious.

Such trivial lessons formed the foundations of focus, confidence and appreciation of stillness and silence which I would need to become a sniper.

Maud married Dad before the war. She was a country girl, a good basketballer. The other teams got out of her way when those legs of power thundered down the court, carefully shouldering opponents out of the way. She was also the greatest cook anyone could find and a woman of endurance. Life was easy in her estimation and she never sought higher glory. Her bulk never changed yet she dressed in a fashion which suited the bulk and always covered up her hairy upper lip. She was rarely angry but when her hackles did rise, signified by clenching fists and twitchy fingers, we all made ourselves scarce, including Dad and the grandparents. If you were in her space when her head went down and those dark brown eyes looked up under her eyebrows, it was too late because she could reach over and deliver a sharp slap on the side of the face.

Dad never did the smacking, it was left to Mum, though it was infrequent. Dad was wise yet I knew Mum had hidden knowledge not often revealed and I heard some of it later in life when her Country Women's Association friends visited. I used to move about quietly (and still do) and stood stock still when Mum answered a question about marriage.

'Relationships are like falling over a waterfall together: one may be stuck on a rock while the other makes a clean breast of the landing.' And then her favourite: 'Relationships can start off all gold and glitter yet in time they can become tarnished. That's why most of us settle for the next stage of gilded, dressed up for the sake of appearance. Relationships are like water, remaining fresh only by flowing.'

Jean, who was her best friend, leaned over and addressed the group. 'I told you all she has many parts.'

The group nodded and Mum's face flushed, I presume because of the compliment delivered by the assembled group.

Ted was like the coxswain on a boat and steered us in the right direction. Apart from some drunken trips on Anzac Day – and he was a gentle drunk – he rarely fell off the perch. He was, however, pinched for drunken driving after an RSL reunion and lost his licence for six months, which meant he had to employ an extra hand to drive him around. Adam had joined the navy for three years and was in training.

Mum's hairy lip bristled like a shoebrush, in spite of her daily applications of Veet hair removal, and it grew until Dad's licence was restored.

I excelled at sports and in the army cadets. My life was full, like those of the country kids at my school. We sledged each other and played jokes, at times we fought and the cane was applied, yet my marks were good.

My friend Blackie the kelpie always sat in my room and watched when I played my war games inside the giant cardboard box which I rescued from the flames of the incinerator and adorned with cut-outs from *Life* magazines depicting battles. There was headroom when I sat in the box. In my unguarded moments Blackie snatched the Sherman tank and could be heard under the bed chewing, growling and rolling it over, refusing all attempts from me to retrieve it.

Once, we were out together roaming around when he spotted a large red-bellied snake. He chased after it. I called out to him and ran towards the small hill and looked down. He lay prone, his hind legs convulsing, and foam came out of his mouth. I looked at his throat and saw two puncture wounds and some blood. He closed his eyes and died right then, in front of me.

I saw the snake slithering away. Without thought I caught its tail. As it tried to swing back at my head, I spun it around like cranking an engine over with a crank handle, faster and faster, and I jumped near the big red gum tree, bashing the head of my enemy repeatedly, over and over till it was still. I yanked out my knife and cut it to pieces and the tears flowed. I yelled out, 'I've got him, Blackie. I've got him,' and then I sat down.

I staggered back home with his body in my arms and my tears were stuck to my face with the red dust which was blowing from the north. I must have looked to my parents like an Aboriginal warrior coming back after a battle.

'Give him to me, son.'

Reluctantly I handed him over to Dad and I saw tears welling in his eyes. The tough old farmer and soldier loved all the dogs.

'We'll bury him by the dam. He loved that spot,' and off we walked later in the night when it was cool.

I helped with the digging. Blackie was wrapped in a clean hessian bag. I placed his Sherman tank and the bits of the snake in the hole. Mum, Dad and I said a little prayer (they believed in God and attended the Catholic church).

'A real Viking funeral for him,' I thought.

Blackie's death for me was a moment when I grew up. My box was stowed away with some reverence as it had been the spike when my life started on a journey of secrets. I grew and my hiding spots grew too – more in number and better hidden. A fork in a tree, a hole in a ground, a thick bush. In stillness, I observed the sounds, watched the mating birds, became immune to ants crawling over my body or a spider exploring, their little eyes bright and unblinking.

Sounds were not totally absent. There was usually a ringing in my ears, a shuffling sound from the soles of my feet, caused by the suction from the arches with socks stuck in my shoes, and an occasional scratch of forearms which sounded as loud as a berthing ship against a wharf. I realised it was not possible to achieve total silence and it was a thought which intrigued my whole being. Still, one must be happy with that thought, I would nod. And, I added, better than death, which would have to be total silence.

Those years of keeping secrets with all of my hidden spots, my sequential thought pattern and my heightened powers of observation lightened my path like flares from the brave French resistance during the war showing our planes the way forward.

My destiny – the military – was locked in like a torpedo fired from a submarine and no stone would be left undisturbed.

The cadets had come and gone along with the Army Reserve unit which I had hooked up with some twelve months before. They ticked all of the boxes and added that I was an asset to the unit with my shooting skills, discipline and advanced bushcraft coupled with a natural ability to assess the ground and, of course, map reading. I was accepted for the regular army and overjoyed. Dad was happy for me, knowing of my ambition, yet Mum was teary.

Adam was home after his turn in the navy on the HMAS *Sydney III*, having escaped a posting on the HMAS *Voyager*. It was agreed that the family farm would be passed on to him and I had no objections. It was 1966 and Vietnam was raging. I would stand a good chance of being posted to the war-torn country.

An unaccountable silence between my parents had existed for months, which was unusual. However, I guessed they had their secrets the same as any couple.

I heard a grunting noise from inside the pigpen a few nights before I left to join up and I guessed it was just pigs rutting. 'Lucky pigs,' I thought. 'I'm yet to be deflowered. Maybe some bar girl – if I get to Vietnam, that is.'

The gate was half ajar and I saw in the half-light Mum bent over with her skirt up around her waist and her head and shoulders face down on two straw bales.

Dad was behind her with his trousers down around his ankles and he was pumping away at Mum, who was groaning.

I stepped back and put my foot in a bucket. 'Shit,' I yelled.

Dad turned round and looked at me. I took off.

I made no comment about it, though the evening meal was silent with the sounds of swallowing, gulping and Dad's false teeth clattering away. Mugs of tea were slurped and the cups placed down overly quietly.

Two days later, I kissed Mum on the mouth and tasted the powder on her aftershave lip and touched her tear-stained cheeks. Her hold on my shoulders was strong and it was hard to break away. I had said my farewells to Adam and my grandparents, who were now in a nursing home.

Dad started the car and we drove off. I waved goodbye. Silence reigned in the car on the trip till Dad opened up.

'Sorry you caught us, son.'

I looked at him and grinned. 'Any Greek in our family, Dad?'

He chuckled. 'No. Look, your Mum and I hadn't been talking for a while – since our anniversary.'

'Is that because you gave her a Philishave?'

Dad stopped the car. He banged his fist on the steering wheel and laughed out loud. I joined in.

'Bit indelicate of you, Dad.'

'Couldn't stand hairy lips.'

'So you both adapted?'

'Yep.'

'Mum's after-five shadow never worried me, you know.'

'You're the son. I'm the lover.'

'Pretty good one, if I'm any judge.' Which ended the subject.

2

Smithy

It had all been done before: the medicals, the tests, the piddles in bottles, the psych tests and interviews conducted with pauses and long looks like a tailor appraising the client with the new suit and the tape measure draped over his shoulders, within easy reach. Then the scratching of notes. It finishes and, judging by the look on his face, it's no use blurting out, 'Did I pass?'

I always wondered if they profiled the aspirants and attached a handle, or was it to test if the fellow was a moron? I wondered how effective they would be if overrun by an enemy and the sergeant yelled, 'Everybody grab a weapon.'

Over the years I tried it out. Once I gave a stupid answer to 'And how have you been?' I replied, 'I think I'm a rabbit.'

'Why?' the interviewer said.

I bared my top teeth and made a rabbit noise.

The same fellow interviewed me in my usual test later on. 'Last time we met, you said you thought you were a rabbit. Any change since then?'

'Big one, doc. I've graduated.'

'What are you this time?'

'A gorilla.'

He sighed and looked at me. 'Why?'

'I can't stop eating bananas.'

He opened up. 'Stop pissing in my pocket.'

'Now you've got it right.' I said.

My boss told me off later.

The recruit course was an extensive re-run of the fourteen-day one in the Reserve. There were a few drop-outs who couldn't cope. Instructors endeavoured to push us to the brink to test our ability to cope with their bag of mind games. Corporals picked on minute details of dress, deportment and leadership. Twenty-four/seven, they emphasised team spirit.

I waltzed through it all and graduated. My parents watched the passing-out parade. Then came Canungra for jungle training, weaponry being foremost. Home leave was granted before we shipped out to the war. The leave was a blur of booze, farewells and thoughts about my virgin state. I put it all aside as I did not need any distractions in the jungles of Vietnam in 1967.

Adam's old ship, the *Sydney III*, docked and we felt instantly the humid heat as it hit our faces like a sandblaster. Induction came and platoons were assigned. I was not involved in a lot of action as we were clearing patrols in an area which had been known as reasonably safe. I saw a couple of our lads wounded by landmines. Another bloke was shot by friendly fire when outside the lines because he had forgotten the password.

There was some R & R and that's when I lost my virginity to a bar girl. She looked like she was about fifteen and it seemed to be much ado about nothing. I never asked her age; besides, there wasn't much time. I paid my money and saw the size of the line waiting. And made a vow that sex had to come with love as far as I was concerned.

The months went along and just before my departure they gave as an exit interview.

'What are your aspirations ,Private Smith?'

'The SAS, sir.'

He read my record. 'Pass A1. Able to work effectively with minimal supervision. Helps other members. Has the highest record in shooting within the battalion. You must take on some other tasks first.'

'Yes, sir.' I watched as he stamped my file 'Recommended'.

I was able to view all the aspects of the SAS course and knew its pitfalls. The success rate is not high and many drop-outs occur. Yet, despite all the prior preparation and the encouragement propelling me, I found it hard going. Team spirit was high and I knew I would receive good marks. However, I found my fitness level needed more work. A counselling session caused me to review my attitude and as a result I put in over a hundred per cent. I passed in third position and was congratulated.

Mum and Dad were not able to attend the graduation ceremony in Perth. It would have been a boost for them to see their son being handed the wings and the khaki beret.

Her laughter echoed across the crowded room – words that reminded me of Mum's favourite stage play *South Pacific*. In my case it was an enchanted evening in the hall in Perth. I turned my head towards the sound and tracked the source and there she was, surrounded by all ranks. The booming humour resounded as she threw back her head, which tousled her honey-blonde curls. I stared at her, running my eyes over her form and it hit me like the dull thud of a mortar being fired. She turned as if on cue homing in on the man in his polyester dress uniform. Her eyes marked me like a laser beam. I straightened my shoulders, put down my glass of half-finished Swan lager and marched towards her in a straight line, my polished black shoes picking up the reflections from the overhead lanterns spinning, twisting and marching in step with my progress.

The band struck up a Johnny O'Keefe number with one snappy roll of drums when I came close to her. I held out my arm and she took it. The cool fingers were relaxed yet they seemed to be in a dance of their own.

The entire hall stood and watched while we jitterbugged together and somehow during that magic moment the universal sign went out to all the assembly: this was a couple who knew one another's movements without rehearsals, and love was in the air. No words were spoken or shouted. I knew I had found the love of my life in an amazing pivotal moment. The band stopped. The cheers went out and we strolled outside with slaps on the back following us, along with the murmurs of praise.

She took out a cigarette and I lit it for her just like in the movies when Bogey speaks to Bacall for the first time.

She giggled, 'What's next?' and her hand brushed the curls off her oval face.

'People call me Smithy. It's Dave Smith, actually.'

'Pleased to meet you, Smithy. I'm Joan Sanders.'

I held onto the hand rather than let it go.

'I see you've done a tour over there,' brushing my ribbons. 'My brother's on the *Sydney*, just come back.'

Light banter continued and over the ensuing weeks I met her family, who were farmers. Her father had been a warrant officer in the war and we understood each other without any dialogue. We were in love and shared our views. An engagement followed yet marriage was held off until I returned from my second tour.

Joan moved to Melbourne with her job after I was posted. She was with the Commonwealth Public Service.

Action with the SAS in Vietnam in 1968 was a different ball game and it became more frequent as we moved silently through the jungles. Some admiration was expressed for an enemy who knew their ground. Their secret tunnels and other spots were well constructed and I knew a thing or to about those types of construction. As a sniper, my role came to the fore; killing the enemy from a secret spot caused me no remorse and I just got on with it.

My first kill was an agent in plain clothes from the South who was distributing information concerning the Australian Army. I hid for twenty-four hours and saw him moving carefully towards the NVRA lines. He looked up in the instant I fired. He was dead before he hit the undergrowth, and silence reigned.

There were many hot extractions and intelligence briefings before another task. I was drawn into the brotherhood of the Green Berets and later the murky world of CIA agents, which honed my skill of focus and keeping secrets. My powers of observation expanded with each silent mission from which I returned unscathed.

One of our US buddies was lost and we never found him. I searched for his name on the long monument at Arlington years later and saw it there. I placed a sprig of wattle from home in his memory. I was observed by some veterans with forage caps and medals.

'Were you with the Aussie SAS?' the older man asked in a southern drawl.

'Yes.'

'My brother knew you. Here's a photo of the both of you.'

I took the photo and saw the resemblance he had to his brother.

'You're Smithy.' His voice broke and I held his shoulders while he sobbed.

'They never found him.'

'I know, mate. It's sad.'

He shook my hand and stood back and saluted me, in the fashion of the Americans, pushing the right hand out rather than straight down. I returned the salute and watched him march away, with his mate with no legs in a wheelchair. Jeez, what a price those guys paid, I said to myself.

We came home and I married Joan in 1969 in a great ceremony in Melbourne. Both sides of the family were in attendance. Dad and my father-in-law became bosom buddies and spent much of the time out in the Wimmera farm after Joan and I had left.

From the moment we were married, Joan became my rock and refuge. There were lonely times for both of us particularly during the birth of my son Shane in 1972 when I was on a course in the US.

Suzie came along in 1974 and I was overjoyed to witness her birth. My life was full. As was Joan's, with her career skyrocketing. My kids were never without supervision as Mum stayed many times. Babysitters were employed. I darted home between trips away and was granted long leaves over the years.

My promotion to sergeant in 1984 had been in place for some time. It brought with it courses in intelligence, bomb clearance and resistance to interrogation.

Warrant Officer Howlen and I enjoyed a drink later.

'Put in for the Seals course in the US. You'll get it.'

'Do you think so?'

'With your CIA friends, there'sno doubt.'

He smirked after the remark and I knew he was part of the secret team. I did not reply but I submitted the application and was accepted.

I had lightly brushed on the huge US intelligence scene. However, after chatting to Colonel Jack Curtis in the US, I was staggered at the resources. Jack was the classic-looking Marine type with the rangy look, steel-grey close-cropped hair and unblinking eyes which looked into the back of your skull and extracted answers without any prompting. He knew my record up and down and sideways. I had served as an agent on some tasks, and I sensed from his looks of approval that I was being offered a position within his organisation.

'That's it, sergeant. You still maintain your military duties, though more limited. A promotion to warrant officer is in the air. Think about it after you finish the course.'

I completed the course and went to see Curtis straight after. 'Will it involve being transferred to the US?'

'No, Dave. We want you over there as one of our agents.'

'I've been asked to assist the British SAS for a short time in Northern Ireland.'

'Come outside. The walls have ears.'

We stood on the steps outside in the cool air.

'I know, Dave, I know. They wanted a sniper and we gave you a tick, as did your boss.'

I realised at that point I was in amongst the big boys and I should forget about ever leaving.

3

Belfast, Northern Ireland

In Belfast, the British SAS squad lay in wait for the arrival of the IRA cell members. The Australian SAS man, nicknamed Smithy, with an impeccable record which included war service and duties as an agent in his country and the US, sat on his haunches on top of a tall building opposite the target area.

He was sent a signal by a mobile phone which gave out two words from the top pocket of his green work shirt.

The officer had an educated accent with a slight wisp. 'OK, Dave.'

Dave looked through the sights of his rifle as the three IRA men knocked on the door of the house opposite. He squeezed off three shots from the silenced rifle which hit all of the targets in the centre of the chest. They lay still, bleeding and dead.

The squad ran over and kicked in the door. An ambulance nearby picked up the three bodies and drove away

'Come over, Dave,' the officer said.

Smithy walked in the open door, noting that the blood on the pavement had already been scrubbed away.

'Great shooting, Dave.'

Noting the captain's look of concern, Smithy said, 'What's up, skipper?'

'Read this, Dave.' He thrust out a report headed 'Australian Government'. It detailed the names of members from Australia serving with the British SAS. Dave ran his finger along the names and there it was: his name, his unit, his current address and missions. CIA connections were included.

'My God, skipper. My God.' He immediately thought of Joan and the kids and how his job had put them in harm's way. He knew he couldn't get out.

Smithy was flown back to Melbourne. He dropped his keys in the hall and heard the sounds of pot and pans. Joan ran towards him, her bellowing laugh bouncing off the walls. She knew not to pry but asked how he was.

'OK, love.'

His curt reply concerned her and she placed her hand on her mouth when he briefed her about the spy papers which were found in Belfast.

'I'm not moving, Dave, if that's what you're suggesting.'

He looked down without reply

'Why don't we just keep our heads down? They could get us anyway, couldn't they, if they wanted to?'

'Guess you're right.'

He spoke to his boss the next day.

'Look, Smithy, we'll make sure you don't go back. You'll soon be forgotten in Ireland. They're Irish after all.'

'Fair go, boss. Some of my mob come from Ireland.'

'Join the club, mate,' replied Colonel Johns.

Joan scratched Belfast off her trip locations and never spoke again about the episode, though she wondered what Smithy had done to incur the hate of the IRA. Then she remembered when she cleaned out the bottom of his bedroom closet and found a green balaclava with eyes cut out. She had held it up. 'Planning to rob a bank, mate?'

He had snatched it from her. She saw him forming words to offer a reply yet nothing came out. He walked out to the industrial bin and threw it inside.

'A man of many secrets,' she had muttered and it confirmed her suspicions about the nature of the duties which her husband was tied into. Was she just like a Mafia wife? She pondered on her question, never daring to form a reply.

4

Joan 1996

I have always been a high achiever: at home, at school, at sport, which is why my friends called me teachers' pet.

Sure, I had many boyfriends and I was at ease in male company, teasing, joking, enjoying a beer with the boys. However, I knew when to deflect them. Yet I could not deflect David Alexander Smith, who rushed into my life like a steam train, wearing his sandy beret at a jaunty angle, which concentrated my gaze on the deep cleft chin which separated his face from left to right. His left cheek bore a four-inch scar – from a passing bullet he said later in the cool clear manner expected of Australia's top soldiers.

The dance settled it all and the rest is history.

My fall from grace is painful to recall, with the blurred lines of high emotion coming and going, fading and frightening. It leaves me with the one constant: how did I get from there to here?

Perhaps it was a blemish sitting in my cells, inherited from my grandmother, who saw the best in all and covered up the glitches, in hope that the good part would override all. I was naïve, I suppose, yet how can we alter our character? It's what we are.

Thoughts flood back a lot more because there is not much else to do between the visits, the catheters, injections, changing wigs, and sometimes I read. The reading helps. Books on dying and what happens after have given a measure of peace to my victim status.

Our marriage, the bliss and the loneliness with his protracted absences, his secret hideaway in the backyard. However, it was a fleeting emotion because we all had exams. We were making our way in the world. Absence makes the heart grow fonder and in my case it worked, though I knew some army wives who gave their own spin to the last word of that old saying.

In-laws are a problem to some people. I was lucky because our two families were linked together like stapled documents. My brother John was on the same ship as Adam, Smithy's older brother. My parents were farmers in WA. Like Ted my father-in-law, Dad was in the army in World War II. Maud acted in the role of Mum after we were married. WA and Victoria are a long way apart.

When I focus on the past, on days when my mind stills and my breathing is less laboured, I remember the time when the crap which followed into my life like a stray dog looking for crumbs broke through a crack in my unsealed aura. I read a lot about auras now.

Work was my second life outside of home and I was blessed with my staff. We were like children sitting on a trampoline enjoying the cushion effect, where we sat comfortable and happy. We bounced, turned, fell and laughed, lost in the joy of just being in the moment.

I have had a slight stammer all my life which did not detract from my popularity, and it did not affect my promotion. I did not consider coveting anyone else's position and never considered the possibility that my stammer would be used against me in a spiteful manner.

The signs were there under my nose when I saw two females standing nearby whispering with cupped hands and sly quick looks. I heard a stammer and then a parody of my loud laugh. 'Hyena' was scrawled on the whiteboard but I chose to ignore it, hoping like my gran that it would go away and they would find another target.

Those little signs occurred in the humid week before Christmas. The damp air hung around. Matches would not strike; towels hung during the day grew wetter by the hour. Envelopes would not seal; neither would stamps stick. Fridges broke down, as did air conditioners, and we were looking forward to a break.

Smithy was away and I slept badly all of that week. He never phoned and I guessed he was busy in God knows what in his spy role, which we never spoke about.

Voices overlapped my dreams; visions came and went. I saw a woman's gloved hand opening my desk drawers. My locker door was swinging open and banging without any wind in the sealed building. A voice kept saying to me, 'Watch it…watch it.'

'Stuff 'em,' I thought and I still bellowed with my laugh at work if something tickled my fancy: I was like the eternal clown who laughs when confronted with the tragedy of life.

Smithy handles all of his problems with his retreats, his tai chi and his martial arts. It's part of his being. I'm sure he approaches all hiccups like a child building a sandcastle. Allowing no other thought to enter the process, he waits till it is built in his sequential style. And like the child whose energies are focused in the moment, he knows he has reached the completion. Something inside him calls out, 'Demolish', which he does and the sandcastle, with all of the jumble of thoughts involved in its erection, is no more.

I can't do that. I'm stuck and I reckon it's all due to fear of failure. Is it brought about by my elevated standards, those which drove me to feel good about myself? My unguarded moments caused my enemies to chip away and weaken my resolve like a small hole in a roof left unattended which grows relentlessly after rain. Unstoppable in its journey of decay.

How could I fight them? The strategy was beyond my understanding because I had never given any thought to the old adage within the Public Service: 'Cover your arse.' It was not on my agenda as I occupied myself getting the job done.

The three people who marshalled themselves against me had a uniting bond, both at work and in their social life. They were always known as schemers yet had never demonstrated any malice towards me. It must have been simmering away like lava deep within them, striking when the gases were right. The mountain opened up and the release exploded over the top and poured down on the unsuspecting victim. And I was it.

Barbara was the ringleader, a person whose aspirations were

curtailed when I pipped her at the post and occupied the highest rung on my ladder. I saw a look of hatred in her eyes shortly after I parked in my new office.

'Barbara, I know you wanted this job. It's not my fault, you know.'

She stood up and she must have been tearful as her heavily applied mascara was dripping from her blazing eyes onto her cheeks. She shook her bottle-blonde head. Her hand was shaking and spilling the coffee on my carpet.

I stood up and said, 'Get a mop.'

'Do you think I'm your fucking servant?'

She stormed out and I was left with one thought, and it wasn't, 'That went well.'

The leader of the pack had finally hoisted her flag and it was a war which I did not welcome

Smithy rang that night and must have sensed something strained in my voice. He spoke softly as he usually did. 'What's the trouble, love?'

I burst into tears and told him as much as he could absorb. I heard him breathing deeply, waiting for me to talk it out.

'She's like Macbeth's wife, scheming to destroy me. I feel it flooding the air.'

'Shall I come home?'

I thought then he would probably kill her. My victim tone had come through. Always the martyr, I told him it was not necessary

Emails became vicious. A contraceptive filled with condensed milk was placed in my drawer and ants scrambled all over it. A black glove with a broken wedding ring was in another drawer. I opened my locker and a blow-up sex doll floated around the office up against the ceiling and was entangled in the overhead fan. The sight of the doll with the fixed expression driven around in circles by the fan and finally being dislodged caused an uproar of laughter and I laughed as well

I drank too much at the Christmas break-up. And in a thoughtless moment I returned a kiss to Andrew my boss, full on the lips. Cameras went off, bulbs were flashing and everyone in the room had stopped talking. Nudges and winks were seen and heard. Photos were sent everywhere and to Andrew's wife, a possessive woman. A photo of two lovers naked had my face and Andrew's transposed on it and copies went everywhere.

Smithy came home and dropped his bags in the hall. I didn't know he had been given leave and I was half sloshed. He stood back and looked at my hair in the curlers I had left in from the night before. I was in my stained dressing gown which had been my favourite apparel throughout the previous week. He was sweet and blamed himself for not coming home when I was distressed. I took long service leave and stayed away. We went fishing and camping, and we made love under the stars.

Andrew rang when we were back.

'Come in.' His voice had a clipped air. 'Read this.'

Which I did. I had been accused of releasing confidential information. There were no guesses as to the name of the author of the report. He concluded it would be investigated and I stayed away. Her report was found to have no substance and I was cleared. Andrew came again with more paperwork He was furious over the naked photos which had been passed around.

'Fill this out, Joan. It's a harassment claim against Barbara Mitchell.'

I felt he was a bit cowardly in not submitting a grievous complaint and on reflection he was typical of those bosses who cover their arses. However, I complied and stayed away from work. Everything was on hold. Barbara and the other two kept their jobs and Smithy was not happy that they were not suspended. She was even filling in my spot for a time.

The claim went on for some time with denials proclaimed loudly to anyone within her space. Something inside my being was lost. I felt like a mountain climber who is about to hammer in the last spike into the granite fissure when the spike breaks and he has to climb down precariously, with the prospect of one final spiralling plunge to destruction.

Four years ago, my armpit was itching and I scratched it and pressed against a lump, which when I followed it with my fingers went into my left breast. Tests came and went and the dreaded phone call from the surgery: 'Come in please, Joan.'

Doctor Bob looked up as I entered and sat down. He made a big fuss of scratching around between phone calls and quick advice delivered in his charming bedside manner. His horn-rimmed glasses were sitting on the top of a handsome head with blond curls. In a place of prominence, there was a photo of his family with three children beaming and smiling. He pushed his eyebrow hair which always hung over his eyelid. (Why doesn't he get them trimmed, I thought.) He struggled to open up a dialogue.

I took up the cudgel. 'Hit me with it, Bob.'

He looked at me for a while and said nothing until he read out the report, which said breast cancer and spreading. I walked out in silence with Bob holding the door and the receptionist giving me a strained half-smile.

It just grew and grew along with my depression and I wondered whether the cancer was the real body and the rest of me was just the lump. I was disabled and miserable and was in victim mode for a long time. I missed my son's graduation from the Victoria Police Academy and Suzie's night of fame with her country and western music. However, Smithy was able to attend both ceremonies along with my parents. Then I had a little good news. It appeared the cancer had stopped for a while.

I was able to visit Maud in 1993 during my remission time. She was in an induced coma after a series of strokes. Her CWA friends were always at her bedside and I could not remember a time when she didn't win a prize for her fruitcakes.

They chatted about their friend and the war years, her with her two sons always scrubbed and well dressed, Ted away in the war and the grandparents helping with the farm despite old Paul being gassed in World War I. They spoke about the dances and Maude trying in vain to remove the hair from her lip. We all laughed at that, adding, 'There was not a bad bone in her body.' She did not wake and just slipped away at age seventy-three. Ted joined her twelve months later and to my sorrow I could not attend his service.

I remembered the time when the men sat around talking about the war, though Smithy did not speak about it in depth. The two fathers and Adam were home as well in the lounge. Maude hated war talk and I could see she was getting anxious. Noises came from the kitchen. Ice cubes were banged to dislodge them, furniture was being shifted around needlessly, cushions being chucked about. Cupboards were opened and doors slammed shut. Probably to lessen her growing hostility, the men suddenly went quiet and looked at her.

She threw her best tea towel on the floor, hands on her hips and glared at the men with her penetrating dark eyes, blacker than I had ever seen. 'You were all kids then. Babies, you were.' Her voice was on the verge of cracking. 'You pretended you were all blasé. Acting out as if you were in a John Wayne movie. Full of bullshit from a would-be soldier who never saw any action.'

No one ever spoke of war again in her presence. She was right. The fashion of her old Celtic genes of women visualising the return of their menfolk flooded her brain. And her contempt for glorifying war, and for the killing of innocents, had come to the fore.

Her funeral came and went and it was a sad affair as could be expected. It pushed my thoughts back to my old Auntie Vi, who lived with us when I grew up.

She was Dad's oldest sister and died just before my brother went into the navy. She was lying in her coffin inside the church. She rarely smiled and her eyes did not smile; rather they appeared fixed like a python peering over a rock. Dad was the lucky one from the old photos I remember because he got the looks in the family.

Her mottled face stared back at me as I bent down to kiss her forehead. It was not expected of me but I complied anyway, as I usually do. It was a new experience because I had never kissed a corpse or a marble slab, which in temperature (I presumed) is the same. I stood up, looked down and watched as her mouth flew open, exposing a cavity full of white teeth which I had never seen. The cavity was a bit of a shock yet I recovered and regained my teenage composure. I once again attempted a kiss and I smelt the odour of brandy, which was unusual as she had died three days before. Maybe she had a few good gulps before she passed on, I surmised.

I recalled as kids we saw her make quick dashes without her wheel frame to her bedroom and then she would guzzle great swallows from her secret stash. (We peeped through the hole in the door.) Her lips made a smacking sound along with the sounds of clothes being pushed aside as she stowed it away. We darted away as she came out of the door with the wheel frame in place along with the grunts and groans of a woman supposedly in pain.

By nightfall, after having puffed through a packet of Camel fags from many given to her by a Yank soldier, she was in good form. The screeching about all the wogs immigrating after the war and stealing our jobs, living on the smell of an oily rag and not speaking English. Her favourite hate was the Prime Minister Bob Menzies, nicknamed Pig Iron Bob, who had sold iron to the Japanese before the war which ended up being fired back at us. After two hours of her hate-filled remarks, Dad would quietly wheel her into her bedroom under protest, with her arms waving and still shouting.

She muttered and snored all night. Then it was down to church at daylight, where she poured out her twenty-four-hour sins to a listener, who could probably repeat them all chapter and verse. Back she went later to the secret stash.

Her younger brother Jack would come in some nights and sing in her face, 'The old grey mare' and she would chuck at him anything within her reach.

And there we were at the completion of her service all with some good thoughts about her: her beautiful embroidery, the knitted jumpers for all of us, and the books which she would read to us. A smell of lavender emanated from the coffin and afterwards at the wake, Dad solved the puzzle regarding the brandy. Dad, the so-called atheist, had snuck a half bottle of good brandy wrapped in a lavender bag just under her left side while she was lying in her last resting place. She had received some sustenance to help her on her new journey (she claimed to have been Cleopatra in a previous life).

They closed the lid after taping her mouth and we all said a few prayers for her. The grog had spilled on the lavender. Mum chastised Dad with the kind of withering look which used to cause Vi to fold up and shut up.

Andrew came to see us a few days ago. It was without his wife's permission. She rules the roost and I think she believes we had an affair. It was a harmless kiss and that is all. I signed a resignation form which I had requested.

'Are you up to giving evidence, Joan?'

I nodded. 'The ambulance will take me there,' I replied.

'You'll win this.'

'I hope so,' I added.

The case was completed and I had no compunction in putting my side of the story.

A month later, the judge gave Mitchell a scathing look and said it was the worst case of harassment he had witnessed. He recommended her immediate dismissal, which occurred, yet at that point I felt hollow and wondered what it was all about. The other two were sidelined to considerably lower paid jobs. I was out and no one came to see me. The Queen is dead; long live the Queen, I suppose, and I knew my time on the planet was limited.

Counsellors came and went and I made a decision to return to my religion, which is a comfort.

My regrets? Plenty of them. I should be at my prime soon to enjoy grandkids and of course my own two. I won't be here to give them advice like mothers do with daughters. Smithy is a strong man yet I fear he will slip into a spiral. I dread the idea of him hunting down

Barbara, which could end badly. Our kids need him more than ever and not sitting in a gaol cell. Do I regret his career which kept him away, and his being embroiled with the agent job? No. I've read too many books and seen too many movies about those matters and it's hard to separate truth from fiction. I've urged him to go to confession. It's not hard to guess what tasks he has been mixed up in. The IRA stuff was a fair guess. However, I can't control from beyond – he must make choices. Better ones, I hope.

5

Smithy 1996

My beloved Joan slipped away from this world fluttering her eyes and brushing at them with withered fingers which had held my hand all of those years. No words were uttered and I doubt I would have heard them as my thoughts were fixed on vengeance against Barbara Mitchell. I had a plan yet I was not able to focus on the specifics. Shane, Adam and Suzie watched and cried when she slipped away. Too many deaths.

At the funeral I stood silent, wearing my SAS uniform, watching the soldier pall-bearers carry her out while the priest muttered scriptures. The family were all shocked and in tears. She was lowered into the earth and I went through jumbled thoughts of our lives, our almost perfect marriage, healthy kids, a cop and a singer flying back to the States soon.

Yet vengeance circled. I recalled Ted's words before he passed on, which for a moment blocked my evil plans. 'A good wife is like great wine. You become adapted to the aromas. The taste, the lingering odours, become part of your expectations. Then you're required to drink bad wine at a friend's house two weeks after your beloved has passed on. You know she was like good wine in that moment. Maybe she's happy. She no longer has to wash your underwear and the socks which you carelessly tossed in the wash basket, still inside out. That's when in one shattering moment you know what you've lost. The echoes of the life you built, the small arguments. The big ones are precious. What-ifs return in spades, such as what if I had made my compliments sound more convincing? That's the overall thought which circles in your head, just like an irritating TV commercial. If she was here now, I'd kiss her twice a day on her hairy lip. Your regrets pile up like a basket full of dirty washing.'

The service concluded and I glanced up towards the small hill and saw a man and woman standing there. I walked towards them and recognised Barbara Mitchell from the court case. I ran towards her. The hairs on my neck were bristling, the scar on cheek throbbed. I heard my kids yelling from behind, 'Stop, Dad, stop,' but I kept on I drew closer and shouted, 'How dare you come. You killed her, you killed her.'

She turned away, as did her partner. And I kept on, rushing now, tripping slightly on a stone. Regaining my posture I stared right in her face. 'I'll follow you. You won't have a peaceful moment until you die, which won't be long.'

They ran off. I still persisted and in one last raging speech I yelled out so loud above the wind that other mourners nearby heard my words and shook their heads. 'What was it all about? Lost your job, didn't you, Barbara?'

And they ran off. Shane and Suzie restrained me and I knew I was in trouble.

6

1997

The complaint by Barbara Mitchell was addressed by the police and regardless of the high emotion which was understandable after the funeral of Joan Smith they were forced to proceed. The prosecution thought a simple restraining order might resolve the situation. However, they were required to move the case which was set down after the usual formal hearings, arrest, bail and the waiting game.

Mitchell gave no thought to the reasons for Smithy's outburst and insisted that the charge of threatening life should proceed. 'He's a dangerous man,' she said to anyone who would listen.

Not that her crowd of former workmates were about any more, now that she was stacking shelves on night shift in a local supermarket. She secretly hoped if he was gaoled she might be able to sue him through the civil courts and top up what superannuation she had left, now that her husband John had left.

John had been unhappy with his wife. He knew of her bullying tactics and bursting aspirations. However, he was a trifle scared because his brother-in-law belonged to a well-known bikie gang. He thought about Dave Smith and how the entire episode had been orchestrated by Barbara. Did Joan's cancer happen as a result of the bullying? He wished she would just accept a restraining order. She kept repeating how dangerous Dave was as if she was trying to tell herself how fearful she felt.

'Why did you go to the funeral, Barb?'

'I didn't want my friends to think I was spiteful.'

To which John replied, 'What friends? They've all disappeared off the radar.'

'So you think he's not dangerous, do you?' Her tone was sharp.

He did not reply and she added an afterthought. 'You've always been piss weak anyway.'

John puffed his thin chest out and his face flushed red. He avoided confrontations with her as she always took the high ground, shouting him down. The anticipation of another court case which she might lose did not appeal to him.

He skimmed through life like a swimmer who concentrates on ploughing through the surface, never diving to investigate the world beneath. John's mind was overflowing with too many memories of put-downs by his wife. It was as if he had at last dived deep and seen another world.

'I'm leaving you tomorrow.' His speech was delivered gently, clear and unashamed and without fear.

Her eyes grew as wide as tea cup saucers for a brief moment until the old merciless tone of rudeness bobbed up and flowed out like a torpedo being released from a submarine. 'Fuck off, then. Go on, fuck off now.' And just to add as much humiliation as she could to her words she said, 'I'll find someone with a bigger dick than yours.'

However, her spite fell on deaf ears, as John was hurrying away in the blustering wind and noisy traffic, his bags already packed and his airline tickets to Thailand in his pocket. Sue, his new friend in that country, where he had been promised a job teaching children English, would be waiting for him in the house which he had bought for her

Smithy stood in the dock unrestrained, being on bail. The facts had been placed before the Supreme Court, where he had pleaded guilty at an earlier hearing. The judge shuffled his papers. Secretly he did not wish to pass sentence as he had served many years in the Reserve forces and had seen war zones at first hand. He made up his mind to make the sentence as short as possible for the veteran warrant officer standing straight before him. His lawyer had tried as hard as possible for his client yet the soldier resisted all attempts to explain his SAS service, though had otherwise made full and frank admissions all along.

The judge was forced to state that being a trained soldier with all the skills of killing it would be remiss of him not to put in place a custodial sentence. He noted that the defendant showed some contrition yet it was not coupled with remorse. The possibility of an appeal hung in the air.

Smithy saw the hard-looking men in black suits sitting at the rear of the court and made some accurate guesses who they were. 'Spooks,' he said to himself.

'You are sentenced to six months' gaol. Three months will be served as a suspended sentence.'

Smithy nodded and replied, 'Yes, Your Honour.'

The judge stood, as did the rest of the court, and left via his rear door. Smithy was led out to the waiting van.

Barbara Mitchell felt some unease when she walked from the court into the fleeting sunlight and looked up. A black cloud followed her on her walk to the bus station. She opened the front door and saw a note from her two daughters, who had cleaned the house. 'Stuff him, Mum. You've still got us.' Tears flushed her eyes and more were to come when she opened the mail from her GP. It read, 'The news is not good. Please make an appointment.' There were no warm wishes from her ex-friends, who treated her like a leper.

A card was sitting by the doormat. It read, 'See how the mighty have fallen.' She washed down a sleeping tablet and went to her bedroom.

Nightmares followed as she faded into sleep. She was in a maze. A desert appeared before her eyes and the parching air took her breath away. Her sweat mingled with the colourful sand, which stuck to her face making resemble a circus clown. She was given a choice by an unknown deep voice: 'You have a choice to keep on crossing the desert.' She thought it said the universe would protect her as it always did. She left the maze and crossed the desert and sighted with sandblasted eyes an oasis ahead with two massive green hedges surrounding a pool of crystal clear water. She ran towards it and drank till she was full. Dates grew nearby and she devoured them. She was in another maze and could not find the exit. Clouds came over and it was soon dark. She sat on her hands and gripped her knees and revisited memories of her childhood. She saw she was the middle child and had to scramble for favours.

Barbara woke up and knew she had been sent messages. She prayed earnestly for guidance.

She dressed and was calm. Instead of catching a bus, she walked to the doctor's surgery. A homeless man came past and asked for a cigarette. She gave him a packet and walked on feeling better.

7

Smithy

My relationship with God returned after chats with the priest, but I had concerns about my sins. Would he listen or did I deserve it? I had to find a way back from the mess and sort myself out. I was not interested in speaking to the trick cyclists.

The imprisonment was not the issue, as I have survived tougher conditions than gaol. The disgrace heaped on my kids was a problem because of my police officer son. For me, it was just a matter of keeping a low profile and meditating. The guards assigned me to a cell with Bill Newman, who had served in Vietnam with his battalion when I was there on my second tour, though I didn't know him. The buzz was about and he sympathised with the conduct which had led me to prison. He told me a few tricks which were helpful, such as getting to the shower while the hot water was running.

Two weeks later, after some sleepless nights and chats with Bill, I headed off to the showers. There were obvious signs which I ought to have taken heed of. No guards about. Two naked, huge tattooed bikies already in the block chatting to themselves at the far end. I had heard they were serving long stretches for rape. During the day they strutted about like the Kapos in the concentration camps in World War II. Their arrogant air followed them along with the herd of admirers they had gathered about them.

My eyes were closed because of the shampoo I was luxuriating in. My focus was on the future and my distraction was obvious and I did not hear their silent approach. It felt like a truck had hit me. Forty combined stones thrust me into the corner. Fat hands held my body tight against the tiles. Soap was flashed on my bum. I felt a sharp pain as an object was rammed in my anus. Grunting sounds, fluid entering and then it was repeated and the pain was indescribable. Blood oozed down my legs and splashed my feet. The agony persisted with each thrust, in and out as fast as a piston. Hands being changed. God, I thought, when will it stop? The yells coming. 'Yes, yes, yes' with each ejaculation. I kept in my tears. God was part-time for me now.

They stopped and I still stood there against the tiles. They hummed and sang a Human Nature song. I glanced at them furtively, while they were lost in their bliss of hot water. A plan formed in seconds. No one except Bill must know of the disgrace but the beasts will, when they meet their deaths. And on their last gasp they will pray for mercy. None will come.

I was shuffled onto a block with white-collar criminals yet the beasts never left my focus. I salivated on what torture they would undergo until they died and what measure of pain they would undergo until my pain was assuaged.

'Smithy.'

I looked round and saw Bill. 'Yes, mate.'

'The bikies are fearful of you– they know who you are now.'

I did not reply yet I was pleased. Let them feel fear, I thought.

I did my time and was released after signing the bond.

I was still a member of the armed forces and no decision had been made about my future. I accepted a trip away on a houseboat to the Glenelg River at Nelson with a group of vets who had closed ranks around me while I was in gaol. The time was enjoyable, although we caught no fish. There were many nights and days when I tumbled in my bunk in a booze-filled zone and slept like a baby.

I strolled along the bank at dusk one night on my own with the thoughts circulating again and heard the distinctive sound of a Harley Davidson. I saw it approaching along the dirt road and it stopped at a shack. The fat man took off his helmet. I gasped. It was one of the beasts. 'Thank you, God,' I said. I looked in the nearby scrub and it was easy to follow the scent of a crop of hemp plants growing well. Soon to be cropped. I knew he would stay for a while.

From then on I made notes of the comings and goings. Ten in the morning and home at six p.m. Paul Thomson had rented the shack, I heard in conversation.

We drove back to our homes and I was not able to curtail my emotions, which were at a high pitch. There was no need to write out the operation order, because it was in my head.

8

1998

He watched through his old green sniper binoculars, making mental notes. The new year had come and gone and the plants were due for harvesting. His hide was constructed of local foliage and on high ground. He slept in a small dug-out and meagre rations were eaten cold in the twenty-four hours since he had been there. Alongside him was the old cylindrical tube given to him by some CIA friends. He opened it, wearing his rubber gloves, and pulled out the collapsible perfectly constructed crossbow and the steel bolt. He fitted the bolt into the frame, checking once again the operation of the bow.

He stared through his binoculars, his balaclava now in place along with his dark tank suit. The old black Labrador sat near the door, occasionally groaning. The dog was frequently kicked by Thomson; it sat up before the sound of the Harley was heard.

'Smart dog,' the sniper whispered as the bike loomed into view.

The fat man fell off the bike and laid for a while in the dirt. He appeared to be drunk. He lurched to his feet and staggered towards the door. The dog whimpered. 'Shut up,' the man yelled while he fumbled with keys.

The fat man was not aware of the dark shape behind but something made him turn round. 'Who's there?' he called out and peered around in a drunken fashion.

The bolt flew out four metres and struck the man in the middle of his chest, throwing him back and pinning him against the door. He slumped, touching the bolt with his fat hands and watching the blood pour from his chest. He tried to speak. The blood bubbled in his throat while he was held like a blinking fish dying in a boat.

The sniper did not speak. He walked over to the dog and reached down, patting him on the head, and the dog wagged his tail. The sniper gave him a biscuit and the dog followed along with each morsel. They reached the car with the bald tyres and the dog jumped in. He had a new master who would care for him at last.

They drove along stopping in little spots on the way. The dog, soon to re-named Ted, adapted to his comfortable home. His new owner changed all the tyres the next day and later on dumped the old ones at a junk yard The crossbow was taken out to sea in a hired boat and cast deep down in the murky waters of Port Phillip Bay. The plan was foolproof. The sniper prayed during the week. 'Thank you, God.'

The police investigation failed to uncover any tyre tracks or DNA. The large crop of drug plants nearby led to the conclusion that it was a drug war or a bikie gang feud. Enquiries were fruitless and the file remained open. However, gang members asked where the victim's dog was. Had he run away?

After the funeral, the members of the gang spoke about their dead member.

The sergeant at arms spoke. 'He used to kick the dog a lot. If the animal's still alive, he'd be happy with who ever has him.'

And the group nodded. He was not the most popular member of the gang.

'Jeez, shot with a crossbow,' one member added. 'Must have pissed off the killer surely.'

'Cops say there's no DNA on the bolt, no footmarks, not even tyre tracks. Must have given someone the shits. The Angels reckon there was no reason to kill him.'

'A careful killing, maybe a warrior… Chuck me another can, Johnno.'

And Johnno did.

9

2000

Barbara Mitchell was prone in her hospital bed in Melbourne in the cancer ward. The cancer had invaded her bones and was spreading. She had prayed to God when the prognosis was declared. Apart from her two daughters, who sat either side, there was no one else and she understood why. It was her punishment, and atonement was foremost in her mind. It was no use going over and over it all; she knew it was down to her own competitive nature, which would never let anyone or anything stand in her way.

She grew to understand why John the brow-beaten one had finally turned on her, fleeing to the arms of a Thai woman, though her daughters wiped him off and would not communicate with him.

In her scratchy voice, which could only be relieved by sips of mild tea mixed with honey and lemon, brewed just like her mother did, she said, 'Did you give the letter to Smithy?'

'Left it in his mailbox, Mum.'

'I really would like to see him. I owe it to him.'

Smithy read the letter and put it aside. He needed to think about it. How could he accept an apology after what she had done?

He once again spoke to the priest, who suggested he visit the stricken woman. He rang the hospital later and enquired how she was.

'You'd better get in soon' was the answer.

He stood at the door of the ward room and saw her lying there with tubes and noisy machines and the two daughters on either side.

Julie the letter-sender looked round and saw him. She waited for a response.

He took a step inside and spoke quietly. 'I can't, I can't,' and walked away.

'Who was that, Julie?' Barbara croaked.

'No one, Mum. No one.'

Smithy walked out into the sunshine and stood, his fingers itching, his head tingling, and he heard a whisper. 'Go back, Dave. Go back. I've forgiven her.' He thought it was Joan speaking and he looked around to see any other signs. He ran back to the ward and went into the room and saw the girls crying and the machine flat-lining. Barbara's eyes were closed

He yelled out, 'I forgive you, Barbara.'

Her eyes opened and a crooked smile creased her face. 'Bless you, Smithy. Bless you.'

She closed her eyes and the nurses walked in and turned off the dreaded noise.

'Thank you, Dave.'

And he nodded to the girls.

10

Smithy spoke to a medium, which was not a course he would normally have taken due to an unshakeable belief that the future can not be seen. A Vietnam vet spoke to him about the medium and he decided to try it out. Her appearance, clothes and jewellery shouted out her New Age beliefs. He thought about the movie he had seen with Rex Harrison and Margaret Rutherford, *The Ghost and Mrs Muir*, and other older ones and smirked to himself when he saw the crystals on the wall and the giant ball on the purple-edged tablecloth. Her face was ringed with black curls and she would have been a smasher in her youth. Emerald eyes peered over the top of Dame Edna glasses. Her long fingers were adorned with a variety of gemstones and her fingernails were so long they could have plucked a hair from a turkey's tonsils.

Her fingers fluttered and waved about casting shadows on the now circling crystal ball, like a phantom harp player plucking at strings. The atmosphere was surreal, and if ever a ghost would appear, he thought, it would be here, tonight. Her beads rattled when they were caught in a sudden cold draft which blew her humungous shawl across her face. She thrust it back. He was sure she muttered in the process, in an irritable fashion, 'Fuck.'

He guessed he looked stressed and thought she might add some wisdom before the reading. He was right in his assumptions.

'Do you know, there is always someone who would gladly change places with you. If you were fifty years old you would gladly accept ten years of being forty again. If you were seventy, an eighty-year-old would look at you as a kid. Bad things happen to good people and it would be Utopia if only the bad died. Look around. Many messages come from spiritual teachers. Sometimes when we are low, I have had people come to me who I knew were so crooked that if they swallowed a nail they would probably shit a corkscrew.'

Smithy laughed out loud. 'My dead wife Joan would have loved you.'

She smiled. However, it was time to get down to business and she rubbed her hands together for a short time, took a few deep breaths and looked at her client. She reached over the small table and clutched his hands. He felt a surge of heat passing along his arms into his middle.

She spoke with her eyes closed. 'Take more care of yourself.' The voice, which came from somewhere in the room, sounded like Joan. His hair stood on end when the booming laughter came out and he knew it was Joan.

'Maud's lip is not hairy any more.' The medium opened her eyes and rubbed them. Her face went pale and she started to sob. The shawl fluttered again yet the windows were closed. She stood up and said in a shaky voice, 'I can't speak to you again…too much blood.' She put her head in her hands and waved her long fingers. 'Please go. Now.'

He walked out, guessing she had seen some of his kills. He looked down at his unwashed clothes and the stains and knew it was an accurate reading. She saw, through the eyes of Joan, his slip into decadence. A sudden gust of wind blew off his baseball cap. He chased it as it tumbled, propelled by something, though the wind had abated. The cap kept on and on, crossing the major road, missing traffic, hitting shopping trolleys, and his breath was running out. 'Gotta get back in shape,' he muttered.

The cap had stopped, edged into a doorway, and was held down by the foot of a tall thin man who he knew, though the face looked mottled and drawn.

'Smithy. How are you?' the man said. He coughed.

And recognition came to Smithy in an instant when the man wiped specks of blood from his lips.

'OK, Bill. How long have you been out of the slammer?'

'Some time, mate,' he said between wheezes. 'The big C finally got me – engine rooms and everything else since I left the army.'

'The vets looking after you, Bill?'

Bill nodded. His attention, however, was focused on another matter. 'Those mongrels that raped you. They're both dead. One got knifed in gaol. The other was killed, down in the Nelson/Glenelg River area, in a shack, so it's said.'

'I heard about the Nelson thing.'

Bill looked at his former cellmate with an expression which was begging an answer. He pursed his lips. 'Thought you might know something about it…'

Smithy did not reply.

Bill went on, not letting go, it seemed to Smithy, and needing a reply. 'Shot with a crossbow, pinned against a door, they say.' His lips formed another phrase. He looked down and away and plucked up courage. 'Raped kids, they say,' he probed, his question still hanging in the air.

'Still, justice comes like a north wind, like the Aboriginals say.' Smithy looked directly into Bill's face.

'Sure does, Dave.'

Smithy ended the dialogue, which he knew had not satisfied Bill. He shook the frail limp fingers as gently as possible and walked away after saying, 'Take care.'

Bill watched as the gap widened. He surmised, based on information he had gathered from ex-army friends, that there went a man who belonged to that unknown world of power. He whispered, 'He's capable of materialising from shadows into open spaces. He has honour yet I wouldn't like to cross him. Have I put myself in harm's way by too much probing?' As an afterthought, 'So what, I'm going to die soon anyway. Rather be shot and get it over with.' Little did he know how accurate his assumptions were.

However, Smithy was held in the grip of forces beyond his control. He belonged to the world of power brokering and the covert monitoring of citizens, the buzz of which had never left him. He knew he was soon to return to the world from which he was powerless to escape. Guidance and a hand on the tiller were marking him for a return, and he was comfortable with the entrapment which followed. Yet there were small times in his cupboard when the word perdition poked its head up. 'I wouldn't hurt old Bill, though…despite his guessing games,' he muttered His assumption circled for a few seconds.

11

The Return

In his office in Langley, the CIA headquarters, Brigadier General Jack Curtis read through a file marked Top Secret.

The one-star matched the relatives in his family, going back to the ones who fought with the South in the Civil War. His career had been mapped out from the day he was born. He removed the yellow tab which reminded him to ring an old Australian military comrade from their days when the two Aussie SAS men attended the US Navy Seals course. Great guys, and their beer wasn't too bad either.

Captain Stephen Howlen belonged to the team of agents which had been assembled under friendly country agreements and led by a two-star general who was senior to Jack. The captain picked up the phone after four rings, which was the current code, and answered promptly, 'Howdy, Jack. Been a long time, mate.'

'Fine, Stephen, fine,' the soft Virginia drawl coming through which led the listener to think of Teddy Roosevelt when he declared, 'Walk softly and carry a big stick.'

'I heard about our friend Smithy. Did some time in Pentridge for threatening life.'

'He doesn't need to threaten, he just does.'

'You kept a low profile, I hear, Stephen.'

'Best, I thought. How did you find out?'

'The judge helps us from time to time. He's connected with our legal service team.'

'Bloody hell.' Stephen never new the full bag of tricks which they possessed. 'Smithy kept his head down. Pleaded guilty, didn't want the lawyer to speak about the SAS.'

'I know, I know. We haven't used him for a while. Thought it best for him to really get over Joan. I sent one of our guys to the funeral.'

'He told me so and was grateful.'

'I'm told he went feral for a while.'

'He's OK now. My mate from the police kept an eye on him. Another vet– but not SAS. A grunt in '67.' A pause followed and Stephen guessed the next subject.

'A job's coming up down the track. Can you give him a nudge?'

Stephen prepared an answer. 'What about the conviction?'

'Don't worry– it's already scrubbed.'

Stephen gave a low whistle in response and was conscious of the power brokering which occurred. 'Don't worry, Jack. I'll get back to you soon.'

Two days later, Ted barked. Captain Howlen walked in after Smithy called, 'Come in.'

He looks a bit older, Smithy mused while he turned on the kettle.

'How are you, Smithy?'

'On the mend, mate. Let myself go for a while, though.'

'Jack Curtis wants you back. A few jobs coming up. OK with you?'

'Is the Pope Catholic?'

Neither man spoke. The pause was like a hawk hovering in the air marking time, studying lunch on the ground.

'They scrubbed the conviction, mate.'

'Bloody hell. The power they wield. It's scary, isn't it?'

'Does it surprise you, mate?'

Smithy shook his head in response.

'Still building hides?' Stephen knew his friend very well. His style of merging, being still, seeking silence and waiting, the best sniper in the country with the coolest head and nerves. Brave, loyal resolute and secretive. Hard to replace.

'Yeah, mate…the bedroom wardrobe.'

'Must push on, then.'

They shook hands and Ted came up for a pat at the front door.

Stephen loved dogs and patted him. 'Great dog, Smithy. Where did you get him?'

'Don't ask.'

Stephen left. He had heard rumours of a killing on the Nelson River. He phoned Jack Curtis, who listened while the phone rang four times.

'He's fine with it, Jack. Raring to go.'

'Good. I'll make contact when the ops order comes out. Might be some time yet. Come over sometime, Stephen, and bring that good-looking missus -- Ann, isn't it?'

'Yep, sure will, Jack. See ya.'

Smithy sat in his secret spot after his friend had left. He knew he would always be embroiled. Mostly, it kept his senses alive, but five per cent told him, 'Can't leave, know too much.' The questions which demanded an answer more often of late were 'Is it in the interest of national security? How are decisions made regarding a state-sanctioned killing? Is it so far down the road that the organ grinders don't have to worry about it, leaving it to us monkeys? Justification: what a word, one which can be used to sanction everything.

He sat in the wardrobe and brooded until he had figured out what to say and something or someone might listen. No use asking for forgiveness. Best attend a confessional afterwards. What must it be like for Father Kelly with all my secrets? The burden of it all.

Still, the pile of unwashed clothes had gone and the area had been scrubbed clean after the first message he had received from beyond the veil. Joan would be pleased.

A flopping noise followed his thoughts. It was like an old wheelchair which had a bump on its tyre; Joan had used a chair many times before her death. He shivered and shook in the sudden burst of cold air which was becoming more frequent and always caused the hair on the back of his head to stand up. Maybe it was an unseen hand brushing the back of his head. The atmosphere was heavy and moonlight sent spears into the hiding spot.

'Smithy.' A cracked voice spoke several times like a vinyl record with a scratched groove. It stopped as quickly as it came.

He sat perfectly still. The sound of his thumping heart beating out a percussion.

'Get sorted.' It was delivered like an order, like Joan did on occasions.

A rose scent drifted past his nostrils and occupied the space in the closet. He waited for another message and the cold air cleared. He sat up straight, his shoulders back. He held his hands upwards with the palms facing out just like the medium said, in order to receive healing.

He closed his eyes and spoke. 'Joan.' He moved his head from side to side as if he could trap her spirit into his body. 'You know what I do, don't you?'

There was no reply.

'I confessed to the priest.' He paused.

'Good.'

He was sure it was Joan who spoke.

'Will God forgive me for my sins?'

There was no answer from the beings in the afterlife, the evidence for which was mounting up in Smithy's mind. 'Crikey. Good chance of meeting all of my victims,' he muttered.

The next day, Shane sat on the old lounge which his parents had never replaced. Ted was at his feet with his head pushing against the police officers's hands for another scratch. His father handed him a mug of coffee and sat opposite. He eyed his son, who had a cardigan over his blue shirt in the manner which spelled off-duty.

Shane enquired how he was feeling.

'Fine, son, fine.'

'You've got to get over Mum.'

'I talk to her.'

'Where for God's sake?'

'In the cupboard.'

'Shit– I hoped you cleaned it up.'

'She told me to.'

Shane dropped his eyes and drained the coffee in one swallow. He looked at his father. Still looks good. Always overseas. Still the spook, I'm told. He remembered the CIA and Brit spooks always at the house. They had one feature which marked them: hard-looking unblinking eyes which did not smile. Joan made up for them with her bellowing laugh and the buckets of food which she supplied and then the men would wander off out of earshot where the serious nature of their work and their deeds could be spoken about. Sprinkled in amongst their huddles were bawdy sayings and discussions about the latest weapons available.

'Dad, you need a therapist.'

'Nup. Got my old army mates here and in the States.'

'The spooks… Dangerous stuff, Dad.'

'Gotta die sometime, son. Hey, what about some grandkids?' changing the subject as he was wont to do.

'Working on it, Dad,' Shane said in a jocular fashion. He stood and hugged his father, which he rarely did, and patted Ted as he left.

He was greeted at the police station with 'How is he?'

'He talks to Mum, sarge, in his bedroom cupboard.'

The senior sergeant was a friend of Smithy's from Vietnam days. He was well aware of Smithy's losing Joan, and gaol would not have helped.

'So what? So do I. I sit in the pantry with Mum's old spices and have a chat.'

'What does your wife say about that?'

'She's used to it.'

Shane walked to his locker and opened it and placed on his tunic. He gazed in the mirror in the washroom. 'Will I get as mad as those two?'

The mirror did not reply.

12

Adam

Dave rolled into the drive in his twin-cab Nissan and offered to stay for a week while my farm hands had some leave. And Ted his black Labrador hopped out with him, after the long trip and eagerly ran around playing with the two farm dogs.

It was a bit lonely on the farm after Mum and Dad had passed on well over a decade ago. I had an important story on my mind which I had written out for my young brother to read later on.

I helped him with his bags and we went into the house.

He looked around. 'Hell, does this bring back memories, bro. Nothing has changed in here.'

'Not even your old room, with your old cubby house.'

He hastened into his room and I followed while he touched the artefacts and I felt he was transported back to the time when he and Blackie played in the old box. His eyes were glazed over so I quietly left him to his memories for a time.

'Got a carton of VB in the back, bro. Want one?'

I told him there were cold ones available and we sat on the lounge. The dogs walked in and Ted trotted over and sat at my feet as if he knew his new name had honoured our father.

'I've got to go to the States on a job soon. Would you look after him for me for a while, bro?'

'Love to. Leave him here till you come back.'

'He'll love the farm. No more snakes about, are there?'

'No,' I replied, remembering the sadness with Blackie.

'Probably won't want to leave.'

I appreciated his work about the farm over the few days and he spoke of how the hard labour over the long day had hardened him up once again. I knew of his fall from grace yet we rarely spoke about it.

'So what's the stuff you want me to read?'

I reached down in between the chair and the cushion where I put stuff (Mum did not like the habit) and pulled it out. I filled him in with a few words which raised his expectations. 'This follows on from when I went to Vietnam a few years back with some shipmates. You remember I was in that area on leave in mid-'65 before you joined up?'

'The postcard you sent is still in my bedside drawer.'

I continued on about the trip in old Saigon I remembered when the war was hotting up with advisers and other troops and started the story when we were on a bus trip.

Dave settled in comfortably with the several pages which I had typed (which I am proud of now that I have embraced computers). He read and re-read some parts of the story.

'Stop! stop!' I yelled to the tour bus driver in old Saigon as we drove along some familiar streets. I leapt to my feet and said to Billy my old sea chum, 'I'll give you a ring soon, mate. OK?'

He waved me away and later told me he imagined there was a face in the crowd which I had recognised…someone way back in '65 when our ship had granted us liberty leave.

I watched the old bus rumble off dodging scooters, bikes and hundreds of people checking out the market stalls. I was busy dodging the traffic as well.

I remember thinking about Bogey in *Casablanca* and wondering what clever thing I would say to the person whose face I saw in the crowd. There she was standing at the corner, holding a billboard and in a time warp which I hoped we might be in together soon. I stopped and stared at her just to be sure. I yanked out of my wallet a forty-year-old photo nearly in bits which had been my close friend for many years. My hands shook and I dropped the dog-eared sepia photo on the footpath. I put my sandal on it so I would not blow away. There was a dusty swirling wind blowing. She glanced in my direction while I was bending down picking up the photo.

I looked at the photo and there I was in 1965 with my coloured shirt, short back and sides and a fresh tanned face and wearing a pair of those Bombay bloomer navy white shorts. A young Asian woman looked up at me with a beaming face, her five-foot slim figure standing with raised toes and sandals falling off the heels. Here was Loan from long ago a few yards away.

I walked towards her and sensed some recognition forming on her face. Her almond eyes gazed at me and were open wide, taking my form in from head to toe. The black shoulder-length hair, still glossy, cascaded in the old fashion. She was more gaunt than I recalled. Still, we had all changed in that space of time.

'It's me, Adam…Loan.' She gasped and held her mouth with the tiny yet strong hands which had bewitched me when I was young.

I held out my arms and she folded into them like two spoons in a cutlery drawer. Her body was as I remembered it.

My recurring dream had cast a sign which I had not considered and the synchronicity (yes, I read lots of New Age books now) of it all was coming into focus. A dream which had foretold a meeting and its intensity in vivid colour, with her small hands massaging my lumbar region, sliding towards my groin, led us into a dynamic act of copulation. I woke up still imagining she was there and that we still held each other, snuggled up cosy and happy. I saw the illusion soon with the fluid from my wet dream flooding the sheets, smelling like a mushroom cellar. The dream was an illusion leading to a delusion. However, on the street years later, it was not an illusion as she clung tightly to my body.

'You come back, Adam.' She dragged me towards the shop and called inside in an excited voice, 'Look after the shop for the day.' She led me to a door two shopfronts away and we entered. There we were in moments of raging lust tearing off our clothes with a lot of lost ground to recover. She murmured low and the lamp was glowing blue, casting an esoteric haze over the little room. It was like I never left in '65.

We consummated our love in seconds, which closed the gap of those years apart. We took a breather while I showed her the old snapshot. She nodded and smiled with the fine opaque skin stretched over her high cheekbones. She reached over and pulled in a shell-frame photo of her holding a child of about four years of age. The child had fair hair and skin. The penny dropped.

'My daughter.' Nothing else would come out.

'Yes. She die when she was ten with malaria.' Loan wiped a tear from her eyes and mine were moist.

I didn't ask stupid questions like 'Why didn't you write?' I did not interrupt as she explained the situation. I let her talk on and by now tears were ploughing down my face with the salt invading my open mouth.

'The war, Adam. I not blame you.'

'After the war, what then?'

'Bar girls not popular because I have a fair white child with an Aussie dad, though they like you better than Americans.'

'Go on,' I said.

She had found a Buddhist convent. 'They were kind. Soldiers left me alone,' she added.

'Your brother the South Vietnamese soldier – what of him?'

'He in your country with boat people. In Melbourne…St Kilda. Got a restaurant.'

'Bloody hell, Loan, that's in my state. I'll look him up.'

Loan had started cooking by then.

I organised a transfer of money for her to draw on. I did not wish her to ever again be in poverty. She had married an older man who cared for her; he had died some years ago She would not accept my offer to immigrate to Australia but I am still trying. I made a pact with her to visit at least once a year. I boarded a plane and watched as her small hands waved goodbye.

I knocked on the door of the restaurant in St Kilda on my return. 'Is Fung about?'

The man entered and we spoke. I had not met him, only seen his photo. A big smile caressed his lips and we sat while I rambled through my history and he his.

'How's the business going?'

'Slowly,' he said.

I reached in my pocket, pulled out my cheque book and wrote his name on one, and entered an amount of $10,000. I gave him the cheque.

He looked at it, incredulous. His lips started to tremble and he touched the back of his head. Then it came out. 'Why, Adam?'

'A debt to you and to honour your family and the daughter I never knew. I love your sister.'

I walked away.

We spoke later on the phone and Fung kept repeating how grateful he was. In my replies I always explained my sadness at not meeting my daughter. My donation to the two folk from the war-torn land was helpful to us all.

Smithy folded the paper and then blew his nose. He realised I also had a love in his life which no one ever thought I would have. He knew I had something else to add.

He spoke first. 'Adam, it's a beautiful love story. I am so happy for you. What's next?'

'I'd like to marry her. She won't leave her country but she will stay here a few months of the year. Would you have any objections?'

'As long as I can be best man… Take love while you can. Don't I know that? Shouldn't have been away so much.'

'Do you think it would have stopped Joan from working?'

'I guess not.'

'Would it have prevented the cancer?'

'I suppose not. Hell, let's change the subject. Get me a VB.'

13

Detective Senior Sergeant Stephen James Ireland adjusted his new glasses. Though they had cost him a lot of money, he often absent-mindedly left them in odd places and was not able to find them when required. Eyes were an essential part of his career, he thought, as he glanced at the pile of manilla folders sitting on his right. One of his family suffered from macular degeneration and was rapidly going blind. She was an accomplished piano teacher and now faced the prospect of her beloved music vanishing. She was left on her own – her husband had moved away before the onset of the blindness. Stephen's parents had cataracts, which also disturbed him. He had black spots and sparks in his vision at night when he drove home.

At age fifty-two his prospects of rising higher to commissioned rank with the extra paperwork involved were fading, despite the high marks he scored in all the exams which he needed to pass to improve his qualifications. And here he was shuffling through the cold case files hoping for a breakthrough – if only to satisfy the grieving. Some of the folders spoke to him because he was fond of getting inside of the head of the perpetrators as well as the poor victims. He cared for the victims, and the loved ones, and the information was frequently updated, in the hope of leads.

He took a gulp from the cup of coffee with the Hawthorn football club stickers plastered all over it and thought about his team, hoping they would do well in the finals coming up. The buff-coloured manilla folder he had opened seemed to invite him in, even though he had had no hand in the original investigation of the killing of Paul Thomson, a bikie gang member murdered in a shack in the south-east of Victoria. A large crop of drug plants was growing in the bush nearby.

He read the neatly prepared text of recent enquiries inside the file. Detective Graham Johns, a new member, bursting with an overabundance of ego and always ready to please, sat opposite, speaking only when asked. Everyone in the squad room knew Graham was going places.

The report was well constructed and easy to read either by a judicial officer or an assistant commissioner. Stephen read the summary, as he had much to deal with. Let the squad read the details, he thought

'Graham, we all guessed it was gang-related or vengeance as you have reiterated.' He studied the photos of the dead bikie. He reminded himself of the gory details flashed about by a press seeking high drama. 'Jeez, shot with a crossbow - in the chest.'

'Went straight through, skewered him to the door of the shack. The body was just swinging in the wind till it was found by hikers – who also found the crop.'

'The bolt was scrubbed clean at the time…no DNA, you say? You believe the killer was a trained assassin?'

Graham nodded and replied, 'Well, it's not the usual method of gangs is it, sarge?'

'You checked the victim's time in gaol. Raping kids, I see.'

'Bloody mongrel. Yes, sarge.'

'Why do we bother, Graham, I have to ask. Justice has been done. Still it is unsolved—the law requires us to put in an effort.'

'Payback from gaol, I reckon. I checked gaol staff but there were no reports made about attacks there.'

'Well, that's a blind.'

'He had mates who were concerned where his black Labrador dog went, though he used to kick it a lot.'

'Any suspects?'

'No, just a clue. A former SAS man, thirty years a vet. A sniper – best in the country. Employed from time to time by friendly forces. He was released two months before Thomson. Funny, he has no record on file.'

'What are you telling me? Where are you going with this?'

Alarm circled the air.

'This is a man capable of planning and executing the killing. The clean record is a puzzle unless there's some higher conspiracy beyond us.'

'Leave that alone. No point in speculation. Right?'

'Yes, sarge. He's undercover, I believe, probably CIA.'

'Why do you say that?' Stephen was starting to get nervous.

'Been in a lot of hot spots with the Brits in Belfast. Then I came into the no-go area and was politely told to mind my own business. Wife died after being bullied and getting cancer later. He did time for threatening the life of the bully. He pleaded guilty.'

Stephen leaned back in his chair. 'Anything else?'

'Got a lad in the job who applied for CIB – Shane Smith.'

'Yes, he's been accepted. Now I know… I met his dad – your suspect. A real-life war hero.'

Graham was anxious to get his last point in. He noted that Stephen was in a speculative mood. 'I checked out his house and saw a black Labrador inside.'

'How many black Labs are there?'

'It was registered two weeks after the killing. What do you reckon, sarge?'

'Any cellmates with this man?'

'Yes, one. Died of lung cancer a while back. Bill Newman, a Vietnam vet.'

'You might be stepping into a very big black hole, Graham. He would have powerful friends, I imagine. Look, bring him in for the sake of completeness.'

Smithy was interviewed about his connections and he explained that Ted had wandered in off the streets. The fruitless exercise came to an abrupt end after a phone call two hours after the interview had terminated, and the suspect was driven home.

Stephen answered the phone and the voice on the other end spoke in his usual coached manner; he was the main spokesman for federal government matters.

'Jeff Jones, sergeant.'

'Yes, superintendent.'

'Well, what have you been up to, laddie?'

The condescending tone with the know-it-all voice that displeased most members of the force. Probably came down from his club where he spent most of the time hobnobbing, Stephen surmised.

'What do you mean, sir?' Stephen replied in an agitated voice.

'Don't take that tone with me, sergeant.'

Stephen calmed down.

'I have just had the Minister of Defence breathing down my neck, enquiring on behalf of his US counterpart why you chose to interview one of our two countries' best agents.'

'Just routine, sir. Clearing up an old case.'

'The bikie shot with a crossbow, right? Bloody good riddance. Unless you have any more than a wandering dog to support the allegations, put it to sleep, right.'

The sergeant did not reply.

'No DNA, no tyre marks, no weapon. Am I making myself perfectly clear on this matter, laddie?'

'Yes, sir '

The phone hung up and Stephen realised the case would go no further. There might be a lone vigilante about but he would make sure there would be no further enquiries. He took the file from the cabinet once again and, with a red stamp, marked broadly on the face of the first page and the folder CLOSED. But Stephen was a careful man and was taught from a young age in the police to cover his arse. He wrote in his own hand in brackets alongside the red letters 'On order of Supt Jeff Jones'. He added day, date and time and shoved the file back in the cabinet.

He saw the doctor that night and was subjected to some tests. The flashing sparks had caused a minor stroke. Tablets were to be taken night and morning and further tests would be conducted. His career prospects had taken a dive.

14

Smithy

Smithy was meditating in his cupboard, which he still scrubbed with Jasol, his favourite disinfectant. His phone rang. He was expecting the call and let it ring four times before he picked it up.

A man with a Southern US drawl spoke. 'Smithy, two tickets coming soon. Can you do a job for us in Boston?'

'What's the weather like in Boston at the moment, general? My bones are getting old.'

'Good. Good, mate. Jack Sanderson will meet you at the airport.'

'Good old Jack. Haven't heard from him for a long time. Be good to catch up.'

'He was in Iraq for a long time.'

'Jack will fill me in on the job, I should imagine.'

'Yes, a terrorist is committing suicide off a high-rise.'

'9/11 stuff?'

'Yep. We're picking you up at your home then taking you to a military plane. Bring that great rifle of yours. Let's do some target stuff later. Stay with us at our beach house for a while. Sorry about Joan, mate. She was a great lady. They're hard to find.'

'Thanks, general.'

Smithy rang Adam and asked how Ted was.

'Great dog, Dave. When do you go?'

'In a few days.'

'Take care. Oh, Loan has accepted my proposal. Are you still with me for best man…in Vietnam?'

'Yes, sure am.'

She Walks the Line

Prologue

Smithy

Arlington National Cemetery, USA

2008

It's two years since I was here, standing with Major General Lincoln at a funeral for another dead comrade. My trip had another agenda back then, which involved a killing, all in the name of justice and security for our two countries and the alliance, an alliance which allows us 'dirty job people' to carry out orders cloaked in the world of espionage.

I'm no stranger to espionage, which began with my SAS service when I rubbed shoulders with the Green Berets in 'Nam and with the CIA. They were heady days.

Somewhere along the way is a bullet, a knife, a crossbow with my name emblazoned on it. When life ends with a painful gasp, I'll be free to face my god and listen to what he has to say about my life. I'm a confessional tragic – the priest's ears must tingle when he hears what I have to say. My priest has provided a conduit to God and afterwards, when I walked away from the church, there was always Joan, my beloved. She understood much about my secret life, though it was not spoken about lest I put her, and the kids, in harm's way. Is the universe paying me back for your tragic death, Joan?

Here I am, still stuck, ready, willing and able to obey my orders, usually a phone call away. It's a habit, because I put the phone down and feel the excitement stirring in my solar plexus and rush in for a shave, carefully avoiding the deep scar which divides my face and seems to get deeper and negotiating the lumps and bumps left after many skin cancer operations.

The phone calls at all hours remind me to stay in shape. As I get older, it's a lot harder. No weights, no personal trainers (who wouldn't know a bee from bull's foot when it comes to killing an enemy of the state), only martial arts, swimming and running to keep my sixty-two-year-old body in shape.

Major General Lincoln walked away after the usual flag ceremony and presentation to the next of kin. It's time for me to distance myself from people saying, 'Sorry for your loss.'

I knew him well. He was riddled with the big C and told me he wanted to end it all. 'Smithy, can you get me some tablets? This is bullshit.'

I would have if I could, but gaol is not somewhere I want to visit again. Powerful forces have worked on my behalf and still do. Yet it comes with a price: it's a pact with the devil, of that I'm sure.

I sit on a seat under the shade of a big sycamore and watch the mourners disperse. I bring out the bulky envelope which holds all of Suzie's postcards since she went to the USA with her country and western group and became a star, and I rummage through them once again. I smile at the memory of when she started as a kid and could impersonate Johnny Cash and June Carter to a tee. I remember how good she was at martial arts – and still is, I imagine, from the belts she has accumulated. With them come the scars, some broken ribs and lots of anti-inflamms to ease the pain. It's not all beer and skittles.

At least she doesn't know about her dad's life and his sniper stuff. Not like Shane her brother, who has got the message, and why wouldn't he, being a Victoria police drug squad detective with snitches who are paid for good info about drug dealers. I fear for him at times, because it's so easy to come unstuck with desperate liars willing to sink a copper and look formidable in the eyes of other dealers.

I flick through the twelve postcards which had been sent each month. My eyes light on Suzie's group in the photo, standing under the Bay City Bridge. She gets around; now in Frisco with its lovely old trams hurtling down the many hills.

I look up again and see a shiny black Cadillac, US flags flapping in the wind on the bonnet, parked on top of a hill. Funny. Why there? Why isn't it down here with the rest of the folk?

I figure it's the president, who maybe would not wish to be seen shaking hands with all the men in black. The presence of those who do the dirty work is always a reminder for him of what they do and thanks to the media he's already in the shit with lots of voters for not getting out of Afghanistan.

There's another photo which intrigues me. On the edge is a man in black with short, straight brown hair He reminds me of Gibbs from NCIS. Late fifties but looks in good shape. He has the persona of a US marine. I study it with my heavy-duty glass and pick up a US flag badge on his left lapel and then see a USMC ring on his left index. I wonder why a US marine stands with her group. Not exactly what a muso would wear. By now my thoughts tumble over like a cardboard box being blown about in the wind.

A stabilising thought comes into my muddled mind. Suzie loved military men. There were always some of them in our house. Maybe it's just a uniform fixation. Certainly her brother Shane had one from an early age. I had one too, from my dad the great army engineer, as did Adam, my older brother, who went into the navy. He went to 'Nam and ended up marrying a Vietnamese woman.

The black limo drives down to the path. The windows are tinted but I'm able to spot a female form just before she ducks down out of sight. Maybe mid-thirties, a trace of long red-brown hair.

The penny drops as the limo flashes by. It was my Suzie. My god, I whisper, 'She's in the US secret service protecting the president. But how? Why?' Thoughts about her impersonations of Johnny and June mingle with concerns about the danger she's in.

I shake my head and speak out loud. 'Danger, danger, Suzie, in walking that line. Bloody hell, what have I done, willy nilly blundering along mixed up in a different world, separated from my family? And now she's in it. Talk about the sins of the father being visiting on the children. But I can't make enquiries; even that would put her at risk.

*

I couldn't sleep for two nights. I made a phone call. 'Jack, it's Smithy, mate.'

The soft southern drawl came through. 'Two years now, isn't it? What's on your mind, Dave?'

I was aware the phone would be bugged, as had been customary for some time in the CIA. 'How's your golf? Can we play soon?'

'Sure. Tomorrow, 0700. I'll pick you up.'

I slept a bit easier that night.

Brigadier General Jack Curtis pushed me into his car at 0700 hours. I was surprised that it was his own car.

'Spooks listening everywhere, Dave. Can't take a chance.' And he added, 'Must have tipped a bucket on someone once.'

We were soon on the nearby golf course engaged in small talk.

Jack opened up after the third hole when there was no one about. 'This about Suzie, Dave?'

I nodded. 'Bloody hell, what's going on?'

There was a short pause while Jack lined up the ball. He bent down stiffly. 'Secret stuff, mate.'

I drove the ball and we walked for a little. 'How was the job wangled, Jack?' I gave him time to think about an answer.

'She saved the president's life from a crazy drugged-up dude. He had an AK-47. She was near the White House gates and jumped him. She took him to the ground and wrapped him up just as the chief's car idled out.'

Unable to speak, I stood there with my mouth open like a gummy shark. But a short burst of pride came to me, coupled with a recognition of the danger of it all. It sounded like a Clint Eastwood movie.

'Bloody hell, Jack, so the chief gave her a job right there and then?'

Again a pause, which was a big part of Jack's style. 'And a bronze medal. She's a brave lady. Just like her dad. You should be proud of her.'

I thought, Jeez, a bronze medal – the third in the US pecking order of medals, but my lips didn't move. I enquired about her band.

'It's an excellent cover when she's on tour. Look, she's been trained in how to collect data. Lots of right-wing cranks out in the mid-west. Many of them crazy and many of them in way-out cults. Hunted down at times by the FBI. All want to kill the chief.'

We walked on.

'She isn't in much danger. Big Martin's an undercover agent and goes with the band when they're on tours. The info they gather goes straight back to the spooks, who sift through it. She breezed through the course, you know. Yeah, and you're thinking about the band and wondering what they know?' Once again the inevitable pause came. 'She's employed as a staffer and when not on tour the band gets compensated for her absence. So howzat, as you guys say in cricket?'

'The guy in black – Martin? Senior agent, I suppose?'

Jack walked on then knelt down slowly again. 'Yep, ex-marine twenty years, sergeant major just like you. Served at Da Nang in '68. He was wounded. Got the Silver Star. Plays a great harmonica. He's a good old boy from Arkansas and, guess what, grew up near where the great Cash was born. I gave Suzie a sparkling report and I added stuff about you too. Anything else, mate, worrying you?'

'Thanks, Jack. Maybe one day she'll tell me.'

'I guess so, Dave, but for the time mum's the word, okay?'

I got the drift. Jack's conversation was never overly long , which is why we get on so well.

1

48 Hours Earlier

The limousine picked up speed and flashed past the rangy ginger-haired man sitting in the shade of the giant tree. His khaki beret was worn at a jaunty angle with an Australian Army rising sun badge stuck on the side which sent a signal to those in the know: he was an SAS soldier.

Suzie Smith crouched down on the left side.

Martin MacRae the former marine watched his companion's discomfort. He broke the silence with a whisper, delivered in his soft Arkansas drawl. 'I know. I know, mate. That's your dad.'

Her hair was much shorter since her thirty-fourth birthday, as if to celebrate her five years with the service. She folded her long manicured fingers, calloused after years of guitar playing

The occupants were lost in other thoughts as they approached the gates of the White House.

'How many secrets have those walls seen?' Martin mused. Among them was the secret of their two-year relationship.

Suzie thought often of the drama five years ago when she was a tourist taking photos of the big house. Her martial arts session had concluded and she was walking back to her digs nearby wearing her favourite blue track suit and Puma training shoes. On that hot August night with the stars shimmering a morse code to all who looked upwards, all her martial arts practice was put to good use, providing her with a life-changing moment. It was a time when her band was doing gigs in Washington DC; it was a very small window of time, the kind of synchronicity Carl Jung wrote about. It was a time when she flung herself through the air and knocked sprawling the insane man who rushed towards the gates with an AK-47. She side-stepped his path and tripped him at the same time and then wrapped him up in a painful twisting of arms, held tight with nowhere to go, until the guards rushed out, along with the president, who jumped out of his bullet-proof limo.

A job offer followed. The band was a concern to her, though. It was her baby and the crew needed her loyalty. 'We'll sort something out to accommodate everyone,' the men told her. The president made similar remarks to her and said someone would get back within twenty-four hours. Which they did. Two men in black appeared on the doorstep of the flat she shared with her friend Joan, an older wiser woman who owned other flats throughout the USA; her money management was legendary.

The agents had a solution. The group would be a perfect cover in its travels around the country. She would be trained how to gather information, which might be useful at some future point in time. The group would be compensated for the times when she was in training; they would be told she was a part-time staffer. It appeared to be a very good offer. She was given a number to ring back as soon as she could. Which she did.

'Agent Martin MacRae speaking. Have you made a decision?' His Arkansas accent was prominent.

'Yes, I am interested. Can you tell me more, though?'

He was brief. A car would arrive shortly to convey her to the White House.

She put down the phone and felt the rumbling tummy which told her when an important time in her life was on the horizon. On the short journey, she thought about her father and wondered if he had just stumbled into his CIA involvement through something very simple. She knew he had started out as a sniper with the SAS because she snuck into the bedroom one day when her parents were out and spied a commendation letter signed by a major general at the head of the CIA.

The driver knocked on the door with the engraved sign which said 'Senior Agent Martin MacRae'.

'Enter,' came the voice from within. A tall man with rangy build, just like her dad but with much shorter close-cropped brownish hair, stood and offered her a chair.

She saw photos of the man in a marine sergeant major's dress uniform with yellow stripes everywhere and bags of ribbons.

'Look, Suzie, the job is virtually yours if you accede to what I'm going to tell you, though I have to fill in some spaces.'

She saw the big file marked 'Top Secret' which he brushed with his strong brown fingers carrying a marine ring.

'Naturally, we've made some checks and you come up pretty good. Are you aware that your father is one of ours? He's served Australia and this country in many joint operations.'

'I know but he doesn't know I know.'

Martin studied the five foot eleven-inch girl with the build of a netballer, fresh clean lines and a great posture. Hands not busy, just like her steady eyes, unblinking and searching his face. They were in the kind of no-blinking contest that he usually won but this recruit was different: she was not going to surrender her gaze and within seconds he was forced to look at the file.

'Have you heard of Brigadier General Jack Curtis?'

'Yep, but he was a major when he came to our house once. Looks like Gibbs from NCIS.'

Martin smiled in agreement and wondered whether Jack Curtis belted the marines on the back of the head just like Gibbs did. Obviously she knew military ranks. He handed her a page signed by the general. She read it and gasped at the honours her dad had received in the USA.

He concluded by giving her a big tick in the box. But the thought came into her mind, 'Am I being embroiled into all this secret stuff and what if I want to get out? How dangerous is it going to be?'

Martin, as if on cue, intruded on her rambling thoughts. He shifted in his big chair and lowered his voice when he spoke. 'Look, we're not asking you to go out and kill people.'

'Is that what Dad did?' And when Martin's face took on a serious look she instantly knew she had lurched into a minefield. A sudden change. No more Mr Nice Guy

'That's classified. So what about the job? Are you interested?' The words had a curt sharpness as a result of her nosey question.

She nodded, having thought it out the night before.

'Very good, Suzie.' Martin leaned back with a relaxed posture. The nice guy had returned. 'I'm a fan of you and your great group.'

She raised her right eyebrow and waited for more from him.

'My accent ought to help. I was born near Kingsland, where Johnny Cash lived. My mother Bea went to his church. She was born in 1925. Ben my dad was born there in 1923.'

'Do you play an instrument?' She knew this was the killer question which could stuff any operation.

'The harmonica. Quite well, I've been told.' Martin waited for a follow-up.

'So I'm told you'll be an undercover agent when we tour, correct? Actually, we need a player so I suppose I'm offering *you* a job as well.' Suzie sat back with a smile, waiting for his response.

'A good point. Bears thinking about. I may as well tell you a few titbits about my family of good old boys. Never had slaves but they were all Johnny Rebs. Great great grandfather Jess MacRae fought with General Jo Shelby, who never surrendered. And never signed the oath of allegiance to the USA. They shot through to Mexico and helped the Mex rebs under Juarez in their fight against the French. They came back and he married. One son named William died in 1935. He'd fought with Teddy Roosevelt in his charge up the San Juan Hill. My father Ben went missing when I was two years old. He was an army man, never wounded but broken in spirit. Another chapter there. So the good old boy is in my blood without the hatred of blacks, 'cos one saved my life in '68 in 'Nam. I'm a godfather to his son. Mum never got over her missing mate but she remained an immaculate woman all of her life. But that's another story. You raised an eyebrow about my father and I can see you're a good listener. One day when we get a moment I'll show you some interesting material about my dad. It's yet another chapter on its own. While I think of it, can I ask you to sign this CD – your latest, I think.'

She cocked her eyebrow and grinned once more when he handed her a pen. She signed the CD.

Martin walked to the gates with her. She turned back and waved with his last words still ringing. 'We'll be back in twenty-four hours.'

She walked to the small Catholic church a few blocks away and lit a candle for her mother Joan and chatted to her about the coming pivotal moment.

The file marked 'Top Secret' was closed but not before Martin added a comment:

> Suzie Smith is a highly intelligent woman with impeccable credentials who has a keen ear and highly developed observation skills regarding body language. She is able to extract information before the subject knows how much he has told her, which is a great skill. I know this first hand because she trapped me into revealing many of my family memories. Her appointment as a part-time staffer/intell gatherer is recommended.

2

Da Nang, Vietnam

February 1968

The operation order was distributed to the officers of the 27th Marines just before the formal briefing. The time had passed for the comfort of the dug-out, with food, earphones and some illegal weed being smoked to lessen the rising fear of death, or, worse, being blinded, having legs blown off. Time to stand up and be counted, to move off with their buddies alongside and the medics following with their needles. 'Up, up' was spoken quietly. No banshee charge, just a silent collection of grim-faced men with camouflage paint smeared on shiny spots, gear secured, their useless vests in place and a last smoke.

PFC Victor Bryon Marshall, a southern boy from Arkansas, was expected by his family to do well just like his father, a marine 'gunny', who survived all the South Pacific landings without a physical scratch, did in World War II. However, his family knew better about the other side of their father. They knew about the brooding man and his rages with the permanent twisted sneer which flooded his face. The sneer was the legacy of a knife wound to the lips in an off-duty knife fight. The bottles of moonshine hidden within an old dank cellar on the run-down farm didn't help his mood when he emerged into the cold from the cellar looking for trouble with his two giant dogs who had taken on their master's habits, nipping and biting the kids if they didn't instantly obey his barked orders.

The children soon learned how to disappear fast into little hiding spots, happy to be away from the large marine leather belt with the buckle inscribed 'Semper fidelis'. But the giant dogs always found them, barking with anticipation of the bone they would get from their master. The beltings came and Victor got the worst of it.

Victor knew he would give those dogs a reward one day, one day when he was older and stronger. It would be a quick trip to a dog's heaven. He learned a form of self-protection which expanded over time into an indifference about death, which was an everyday occurrence on the old farm. Best not to get too attached to an animal or a sister who might betray you, best not to care about death or cold. His indifference was extended to most people he knew, though he had a certain amount of affection for his younger brother Mark, who adored him. The only other exception to his rule was himself.

He feared death and the demons which would follow. Death had a smell which he quickly found out and when it came he would cover his head with an old grey greatcoat which belonged to an ancient uncle who had fought under the tigerish General Nathan Bedford Forrest, who also rallied the Ku Klux Klan in 1866.

One hundred and two years later, he sat paralysed with an old coat over his head, away from the smell of nicotine which reminded him of the yellow-stained fingers and breath of his father. Victor had signed up and Parish Island boot camp loomed. Among his last few acts before he left for the marines was the drowning of the two dogs in the dam after he'd lured them there like the Pied Piper. His father suffered the same fate with a quick push of the boot from his son. There was no coroner's inquest. Just a quick burial and peace for the family. Only a few old vets recalled what a good marine he had been.

*

The bullets whizzed around outside the trenches and there were dull thuds and metallic whistling sounds which sent fear among the men that mortars might pick up the scent of the humans. 'Just like the dogs,' he murmured. But the stupid officers were blowing whistles and yelling, 'Out, out.' The artillery barrage had started.

It was different from the training. This was real. He wanted away from it all. Away from the nicotine. A plan came in an instant. The troops lumbered up. He pushed away the old coat and stood with his M16 held out pointing to his head. He pulled the trigger and the sear on his right temple caused him pain, not deep yet enough to cause blood to flow and blackness to follow.

The general walked around the MASH tent shaking hands with the wounded men, taking care if some of them had no arms. He bent down and pinned a Purple Heart on Victor's pyjama coat. He shook his hand and moved on.

Victor smiled to himself in the night at the thought of how clever he was.

However, his foxhole partner PFC Martin MacRae didn't smile when he came to visit when the choppers loaded them all for a flight back home. Victor knew he had not fooled Martin and from that moment a seed of hatred was formed in his mind. Like dogs, nicotine and drugs: they would all be obliterated from his presence, given time.

The less wounded marines were flown to Sydney for R&R leave. Victor met a nineteen-year-old girl in a bar who was dazzled by his uniform and the small purple ribbon. They went to a hotel nearby and had sex. He wrote his name – Martin MacRae – on a piece of paper and laughed as he walked out, soon to be back in the USA.

Yvonne Streeter was sad about the loss of her virginity but treasured the note with his name scrawled on it: she kept it in her small musical jewel box with the ballet dancers circling around. She loved ballet.

Victor never knew that Martin forgot about the minor injury because of the mounting casualties of the battle scattered about the Da Nang airbase. Martin was not a judgemental person. He was a happy man who entertained his buddies with a harmonica.

Martin stayed happy despite being severely wounded two days later. He lost one testicle and a portion of the other. He maintained a positive disposition though the loss caused him some quiet inner trauma. When the dark thoughts came, he would pick up the harmonica and play it endlessly till the emotion went away. The Silver Star which was awarded to him as a result of his actions in the battle remained sitting quietly beside the hospital bed. Every now and then a high-ranking officer who was visiting asked if he could see the medal. After all, it was the second on the scale of honours given by a grateful government.

Martin was recruited into the Secret Service in 1991 at the age of forty-one after twenty-three years of continuous service in which he rose to the highest NCO rank of sergeant major of marines. At his retirement show, an indelicate marine fuelled with gallons of beer shouted out, 'He's a Russian, you know. Ivor Knackeroff,' which caused a silence to descend on the hall.

*

Victor wormed his way into the Washington city police and became supposedly intent on destroying the drug trade. He worked close to Martin's workplace but they never met.

3

USA

2006

Martin pondered for some time how to tell Suzie about his war injury. They had at that time not made love, though the prospect was circling in the air and a decision to speak out soon was appropriate. After all, she's young enough to have children and I'm no use in that area, he thought.

'We're getting along fine, mate,' (he called her mate on many occasions) 'but we have to be careful. The rules.'

And she would always reply with the same words, 'Yeah, no fraternising. It's laughable, really, when I think of all the shagging going on in the halls of power, right under the noses of the bosses who made the rules.'

Martin recognised how forthright she was and admired her for it – something to do with the Aussie spirit and he had a fondness for Australians. He looked down deep in thought.

Suzie studied his face when he was thoughtful and knew that words were sometimes stuck. He licked his lips before speaking.

Maybe it's a moisture thing, she mused. 'Spit it out, Martin. You're a hawk, boy, not a chicken.'

He laughed at her imitation of a favourite cartoon. He produced an old dog-eared medical photo in which she saw a twenty-year-old Martin on a hospital bed with a bandage around his groin.

'Mate, I lost a testicle and part of the other at Da Nang. Can't have kids. Haven't tried to make love for years but it wasn't a problem once.'

'So what are you trying to tell me, Martin? Maybe that you're not a complete man? Please don't hand me that crap.'

Martin persisted. He did not wish for her to be under any illusion. 'But kids. You're young enough, you know.'

She jumped straight in with a matter-of-fact answer. 'Listen to me, Martin. They're not on my radar. Kids are out with me. So what's your next line?'

His last words on the subject, which he had feared to raise for a long time, poured out in a rush. 'I'm able to get it up. Viagra will help later, so the smart quacks say.'

Suzie finished his worries with the great big radiant toothy smile which surged all over her features. 'So it's Viagra. So what?' She patted him on the shoulder and stared into his face but without speaking for the moment, sensing that Martin wanted to have the last word, which he did.

'Hell, I am glad I met you. I love you but I was too scared to tell you. It's been a struggle.'

'Me too. I love you heaps but let's not rush it for the moment, Martin. Is that OK with you?'

Martin started to giggle and knew then he ought to tell her something else. 'Someone gave me a blow-up job which fits over in cases of emergency. It has a blow-up tube on the side which the partner can pump up.'

Suzie started to giggle and it was still in her voice when she asked another question. 'What if I pump it and it keeps going up?'

'I guess I'll have to scrape you off the ceiling.'

She started to laugh and Martin hushed her. 'Watch out. Someone's coming. They're good at body language too, you know.'

4

Suzie

2008

I looked many times at the old photo of Martin's family in his flat, not far from where I live. It was either laid flat or stood up, depending on the mood he was in. His sister Jane, who beat him to Vietnam in 1966, was a MASH nurse in Saigon and later married a surgeon. She lives in Baltimore and still works. There has been sadness in her life – she lost her only child with meningitis at the age of eleven and nobody speaks about it.

I was staring at the separate photo of Jane, Martin and their mum Bea when I heard Martin walking towards me. He looked at the photo.

'She looks sad in this shot, Martin. I guess it was after the loss.'

'Yes. It was an unhappy time. She and Bill nearly parted but they're OK now. They ought to be after all of those years together.'

'It's another reason why I don't ever want to have a child The loss of a child would be the greatest nightmare.'

We watched a re-run of the *West Wing*, which is a prerequisite for White House staffers.

Later there was a quiet moment until I spoke. 'Would you like to talk about Bea? I know she died in 1990. I'll get us a drink.'

'It might be a bit long-winded, you know.' He tapped his knee, concentrating on how he would start, and the easy drawl came out. 'Mum went into dementia rapidly. It was a hit and miss affair with lapses of memory and haunting expressions. Words didn't connect, which was sad for her because her grammar and sentence construction were very good. Shoes frozen to useless were found in the fridge and she'd gaze for hours at her wedding album. She lost her lifetime job as a waitress when she tipped a bowl of spaghetti over a grumpy customer. He sat looking like a sheepdog caught in the rain, his eyes bolting like a meerkat which had swallowed a golf ball. The staff were sad to see her go. She made an eloquent speech spliced with humour which had them rolling in the aisles.

'Jane watched her closely from then on. She loved dancing and always trotted around to Fred and Ginger – without clothes when the rot set in but we didn't know that until she opened the door to the mailman and signed for the mail, with him standing there dumbstruck. She wished him goodbye and closed the door. We were in fits when he told us about it.

'Jane caught her pushing a turd around the bath and talking to it at the same time so she found a respite home for her. She had a good nurse named Angela. She was only fifty-nine, which was too young.

'Jane said she used to have a lot of fun when Dad was still with us. He'd get on his high horse about something and jump about restlessly. Bea would watch and call out, "Left turn, Ben, now right turn, Ben, about turn, Ben," and he would stop, realising how stupid he looked.

'Anyway, Jane and Mum and I got on with our lives as best we could, with me back in the marines for a few more years, until the police contacted Jane saying they had found some old remains in the mountains. There was a tape in the rotten clothes and it was Dad signing off in his last moments. He'd been crushed by a giant boulder. We identified the remains and were sad at how Dad had come unglued before he left and after.

'We made a choice to let Mum listen to the tape so we took it to Angela. Mum's ears pricked up. Our mum of old returned for a brief time. She recalled her feelings before the separation, feelings which had been stuck in the archives of her mind. She remembered how she had focused on the care and protection of her family. Memories of her wedding and anniversaries came back to her.

'She accepted that her health was failing but she revelled in the words on the tape, which brought her some long sought-after closure and peace. She vowed to make the best of the years she had left. And no one could ever prise the tape off her after that. It became her teddy bear and sat alongside her in her sleep. Angela's a medium and she was sure a male voice came through the teddy bear at times in the night. The tape went with her into her grave.' Martin paused.

I had held my breath right through the sad yet wonderful story. His eyes were glistening and I wondered whether it would be appropriate to ask a few questions.

'When did she die, love?'

'1990. She and Ben were buried in the same grave.'

'Did you make a copy of the tape?'

Martin nodded.

'Can I hear it now?'

The phone interrupted us. It was the White House. Some paperwork had to be fixed.

'Some other time, mate. I don't feel up to it. Gotta rush out.'

We're no different to any other people on the planet and spoken words are easily forgotten. We should write them down or record them like Ben's tape. In his last moments he was obviously able to get the message out to his loved ones.

5

Suzie

2009

One of my better choices with regard to the band was to recruit a gifted keyboard player. She was Joan Oliver, my flatmate. Apart from her skills, which she also taught me, she shared my mother's name. She looked a bit like her too, with curls around her oval face. And best of all she sang like Joan Baez, one of my favourite folk singers. She wasn't liked in parts of the South 'cos she went on the marches and the freedom rides with Martin Luther King. I was aware of that on my tours in the early days and always careful with my speeches on stage.

However, Joan was unlucky in love because of the choices she made in men. Most of them were snorting cocaine every chance they got and spending Joan's money – she was wealthy thanks to her interest in real estate and accountancy. In time the gamblers got the flick.

She also hated smoking, because the smell of nicotine made her sick. It was that which eventually attracted her to another good old boy and former marine named Victor Marshall, who apparently had been wounded in 'Nam. He hated smoking. He was a Washington police detective around her age. Never married, no kids and quite wealthy, a bit of a surprise for a cop. And from Arkansas. I wondered whether Martin knew him but let it go. The less talk about us two the better.

I have an instinct about some people. I either like or dislike them; there are no in-betweens. In Victor's case I disliked him intensely. He was fond of bragging about the Purple Heart he had been awarded in battle. Martin, my dad and my Uncle Adam rarely ever speak about their medals.

My affinity with some groups extends to cops. My cousin Rosemary was an Australian federal cop until she was wounded in Afghanistan. She came out a hero after saving a child's life on a dusty road. She almost lost a leg in the explosion. She's now invalided out and married to Westie, a war correspondent who was at the scene of her bravery and wrote about her. I have a copy of her letter with the newspaper cutting about the action she was in. She was given a medal and now illustrates children's books where she lives in Canberra. And then of course there's my brother Shane, who is a Victoria drug squad detective.

Marshall's traits were obvious. He was a sleaze, but Joan would hear nothing bad about him. From what I picked up, the sex was good so in that area I guessed they might make it. Her only child Annette lived with a healer in Brazil, which Joan did not approve of. Joan is agnostic. Not like me, who talks to God or whatever spirit comes through. My mum comes through at times. I've not seen her full-on but hope I will one day. She appears in dreams and frequently sends messages like 'Watch Marshall'. However, I just turn over and go to sleep. How could I tell Joan about a message from beyond? She would just laugh.

Until the day I was woken up by a disturbing phone call from the local hospital. Joan had been bashed and wanted to see me. I scratched off a note to Martin and fled out the door.

Her face was puffed around the eyes and black bruises were showing up, yellowing at the edges almost while I watched.

'Don't tell me, Joan. It was Victor.'

She nodded with a painful move of her head.

'Why?'

'We had a blow-up. He wanted access to my bank deposit box and I refused.' Joan groped in her handbag and produced a a duplicate key, and asked that I keep it. She added, 'My will is also in the bank box. You're written in it with my daughter Annette.'

'Stop, stop. You're not dead. You're going too fast for me.'

She looked at my face just like Mum did and read my next response, just like Mum would do.

'No. Not going to the cops. I just want him out. They wouldn't believe perfect Victor the non-smoker could be a crook.'

I was intrigued by the remark about him being a crook and she saw the question on my lips.

'Yes. He's a big drug dealer. Can't stand druggies but doesn't mind fuelling them.'

'How do you know he is?'

'Phone calls all hours, creepy people banging on the door. And then I spotted a stack of coke in his car.'

She was exhausted by all of the emotion so I left her quiet and headed towards the cop shop.

'Where is Victor Marshall?' I demanded from the young cop. I showed him my White House staffer's pass and he almost jumped to attention, calling me 'Ma'am'.

'Cut the crap. Get me Marshall now – right now.'

Victor came to the counter all silly smiles. 'What's up, Suzie?'

But I wasn't in a smiling mood. I was in a rare rage at that point and would have hit him if he'd stepped too close. 'Don't call me Suzie. Come outside.' Outside, I went on, 'You're fucking lucky she won't press charges. Stay away or I'll get some high-powered people to fix your wagon.'

'Oh, oh, I'm so scared of big White House staffer.' He turned away, walked back into the police station and lifted his middle finger at me.

I watched the arrogant walk and thoughts pounded in my head like 'Mate, you have no idea what I'll bring down on your head, you arsehole.'

*

Victor went back again and bashed her. She reported him to the police and told them the whole story. They found masses of drugs in his unit. He was arrested and charged. When I told Martin about Victor, he remembered him from 1968 but hadn't been aware of his police career.

We sat together in the court when Victor was sentenced to a long stretch. He was about to be propelled out to the cells by the guards when he looked up to where we sat and saw us three. It must have dawned on him that Martin and I worked together. He probably knew what Martin's secret role was. Probably made enquiries, unbeknown to Martin.

'Fucking dogs,' he yelled when they carted him away. 'I'll kill you' were the words on his lips as the cell door was slammed shut.

A man in a crumpled suit sitting in front of us turned round and studied our faces. I instantly felt the danger and the revolving gut. I scratched the top of my itching head and knew by the features of the man that he was a close relative. He turned out to be Mark Marshall, Victor's younger brother. A person of interest; a man with a mission.

Joan's breast cancer began that year during the terrible time.

6

Suzie

2014

My fortieth birthday has come and gone. It was a good show with Joan and my friends. I hoped Mum might show in spirit but I'm still waiting. Maybe she's gone on to some sort of parallel dimension.

Forty is dreaded by some, yet a milestone for others. It was a huge milestone for me after ten years on the White House staff and all the madness which went with it. My, where did it all go? I thought many times. So much has happened but it's nothing in comparison with the Earth, which was still able to circle the sun ten times, despite all the dire predictions from the many cranks I met on my tours.

I know there's an ending soon to this life of secrets, especially with Martin, and I duck about wearing out shoe leather, wasting petrol and pushing aside little hints from people who are suspicious, hoping for a little gossip to make their day happier (until the next breath of scandal). I've witnessed many so-called scandals which have ended in tears and walking away from a good career. Another president is looming on the horizon and may not appreciate what I did ten years ago.

I'm still held in the grip of the forces of espionage, forces which are beyond my control even though I was a minor partner in that world of brokering, coupled with covert monitoring of citizens, the buzz of which has never left me. But its main thrust was the right-wing crazies who wish to harm the chief. Dotted among all of that mess of disconnected wires and disconnected people were the benign ones and the malignant one, and I have encountered both.

Yet it's not easy to leave that world behind and forge ahead to something else. I'm comfortable with the entrapment which has topped up my bank balance for many years. The ride has been good, generally speaking, and I didn't have to participate in any kills, or give evidence in any commissions of inquiry. In spite of what you see in the movies, intell can be very boring. My job was just the steady collection of information for the back-room boys, who made what they could out of it all, turning some of it into intelligence.

I currently crave another tour to Nashville and other places with Joan, who wants to make it her swan song before the lump becomes the body and the body disappears, leaving its malignant double. Above all, our plan is to be married this year, with Joan as my matron of honour. Martin can at least continue, relaxed about not being found out. He's coming with us on the last tour before I leave and has brushed up on his harmonica.

Don't know where those days went but the group are on the stage setting up in Nashville. I'm about to walk out. The crowd are foot-stomping and many are boot-scooting in the aisles, much to the anxiety of the security staff. There I am with my big John Cash black outfit and my twangy guitar. The crowd know what's coming and I don't keep them in suspense when I launch into 'I hear the train a coming, a coming round the bend, and I ain't seen the sunshine since I know when I'm stuck in Folsom Prison'. I hardly hear the rest of my words and hope I've got his quiver right. Number after number goes on. I stop for a while and drink a lemon squash and honey mix.

I save one of my favourite writer-singer's songs to the last. I say 'Joan Baez' and the sound is deafening. Maybe they've got over the freedom rides.

'The night they drove old Dixie down.' Silence took over the hall. I looked at the faces of men and women wearing Rebel hats and knew I was on a winner. 'Virgil Caine is the name' and then I went on with 'And the bells were ringing'. Many of those giant good old boys were sobbing as if they had been at the small house when General Robert

E. Lee surrendered his army of Northern Virginia to the scruffy but brilliant U.S. Grant.

There were more tears when Martin strolled out in his brilliant coloured marine blues with all his medals and played his harmonica to the old Reb martial tune 'The Bonny blue Flag'. And the audience quite remarkably knew the words and sang.

We left the stage but were called back for an encore. Martin started me off with the harmonica and I started to sing, 'I keep a close watch on this heart of mine. I keep my eyes wide open all the time.' I finished with 'I walk the line' and I confess that when I bowed I was caught up in the moment, with the tears flooding down. It was the last round for Joan and I asked her to stand, which she did, to another round of applause. We had to leave just after.

I resigned when I was back in DC. I was tearful because I had made many friends and a lot of them were coming to the wedding. Many of them had guessed about us, but to their credit they kept their mouths shut.

It is the wedding and we stand in the small Catholic church. Joan is my matron of honour. We picked 'Stand by your man' and then the marines' hymn and walked out with laughter and happiness following us. I wished Dad could have been here but he's suffering from a broken rib (a martial arts injury, of course).

Joan had two weeks to live. She had hung on by the skin of her teeth just like the biblical Job said. She died and many bands were there to send her off into her agnostic plane. She was happy to go, she told me through pain-racked lips. Joan was great lady, a great muso and my surrogate mum. Annette was there and I showed her the will. The two had reconciled well before the funeral.

A decade-long chapter of my life had closed and I looked forward to another time. It came in 2015.

Martin works a few less hours of late and I still have my gigs. Dad is better and we talk a lot more via email. Although he won't say anything in the text about my last career, I knew that he knew, in some fashion, after the funeral in 2008. We leave it at that. Once we get to Australia, and out of bugging range, we can chat about it.

I'm excited about my trip back to Oz. I can't wait to meet my nephew Michael with his dad Shane and his mother Teresa, my sister-in-law. Haven't seen her since Dad went off his rocker at Mum's funeral and later on went to gaol. But that's another story.

7

Suzie

Australia

Dad met us both in Perth for a reunion with his old SAS mates. It's where he first met Joan, who was a Perth girl, daughter of a warrant officer and a farmer just like my grandad Ted, who was an army engineer and also a broad-acre farmer.

Adam my uncle was there with his Asian wife Loan. I hadn't seen him for years; he had aged and his face was lined but his body looked lean and hard. He had giant farmer's hands just like his father. Not bad for a man in his mid-seventies.

Dad picked Martin up for a day at the RSL. The old men loved him and asked him about the middle east wars – he had some views about why we should be there and when we ought to pull out. He was shouted so many Swan lagers that Dad had to pour him into the car, where he fell asleep on the way back. He snored all night, waking up with a great headache caused by the heavy Australian beer.

The president of the RSL invited him back to speak. He was highly regarded by the old diggers, some of whom had fought in Vietnam with the marines. So much for my concern. I realised that Martin had studied politics and accepted other people's views and countries.

In his talk, he showed some slides of Da Nang and other places of interest. He was warmly welcomed and cheered at the end of his short speech. I'm sure he assisted in propping up US–Australia ties. He declined the offer of more Swan lager and stayed with Margaret River white wine, some of which he brought back. So we both ended up with headaches. Dad was proud of him, as was I. I had made a great choice in a husband and protector after all those years.

The drums sounded into the corners of Perth and it was clear that the message had got out. Home-town Aussie girl Suzie Smith was in Perth. The hall was packed.

There was a hint in Dad's voice the day before. 'Take your instruments. There's a band there, OK.'

I briefed the band about what I'd sing and they agreed.

I called to Martin. 'How many out there?'

'It's packed,' he replied.

The band leader announced my appearance. I walked in and bowed in a sweeping Peter Allen outfit with an Aussie shirt. I loved Peter, our icon, as did Broadway, and I'd practised his tunes for many years. I'd had piano lessons with Joan Oliver.

I sat at the piano and began 'I still call Australia home'. The chorus went on, with the audience standing and singing and crying along. I went into 'Tenterfield Saddler', Allen's signature song, and after the noise settled I sang the song made famous by Melissa Manchester, 'Fly high and wide', and then Peter's 'I am not the boy next door', his song about being gay.

I looked at Dad in the front row. He was wiping his eyes, along with Adam and the rest. More Johnny Cash and June Carter songs were sung until I had to take a break.

Martin strolled out in his marine dress blues, harmonica at the ready.

'Ladies and gentlemen, this fine-looking sergeant major of marines is my husband and he plays a mean harmonica.'

The audience cheered. Many of them would never have seen a senior NCO of marines in full dress.

Martin had a voice not unlike Elvis. He started to play the famous number when Elvis sang the combination of Dixie and the Battle Hymn of the Republic. We played along with him in the breaks when he blew and sucked into his harmonica. He then played and sang 'God

Bless America', followed by 'Advance Australia Fair'. I'm sure many of the females in the audience would have abducted him if it were possible. I rounded off by coming out in my big John outfit and sang 'I walk the line'.

It was over and I had a sore throat to prove it. But there were autographs to sign and CDs to sell. I was busy with the fans but noted that Martin's fan club was swarming around him. I knew he was a chick magnet but the surging crowd were starting to scream. Some were touching his uniform, and clutching hands ripped a badge off his collar.

My fans were drifting away and it was then that my eyes locked on a woman about Martin's age. She was staring intently towards me and I of course went into my non-blinking routine. A woman who I judged to be around mid to late forties was with her and their looks were similar. I guessed she was the daughter. They both suddenly turned about and walked off, but the face of the older woman stayed in my mind for a long time. Her expression was not one of kindness and indeed I felt some hatred drifting towards me. My tummy started to rumble and I knew in that instant she would bring danger somewhere along the track.

We had never discussed fame and its effects. Like most people, Martin had no idea of celebrity status and the sting in its tail. That was my cross to bear, not Martin's, until now. People want to know the famous person yet it is only to corroborate their own imaginary image, their perception of themselves. Poor Martin. He doesn't know how dangerous it is. He doesn't know how many fans would like to bring their idol down. Good old friends and family who know your flaws provide the checks and balances and are the answer to fame. Not the agents or the herds of emotional sponges who gather like vampires and suck the marrow out till nothing is left and even the bones are consumed.

8

Suzie

Melbourne

The farm boy in Martin came out when we entered the expansive property in the Wimmera district of Victoria. Dad had driven down with us as well to stay with his brother Adam. Loan had flown back to Vietnam. The two had an arrangement in which she stayed alternative months with Adam and during that time cooked masses of great Vietnamese food kept in containers in the giant freezer. I sampled some of her cooking when we first arrived and I'm hooked forever on Asian food. Martin is easy peasy but generally he's a meat and potatoes man.

I still can see the look on Martin's face after he asked Adam how big the property was.

Forever the laconic Aussie, even more so than Dad, who is usually 180 degrees, Adam replied, first taking off his usually fixed bucket hat and scratching the back of his head. 'Ten thousand acres.'

I held Martin's right arm because I thought he'd faint.

'Holy mother of God,' he breathed and just shook his head.

I helped him through his wonderment. 'This is dry land. He needs that much for a big broad-acre crop. Wheat, barley, oats, lots of canola and some lucerne as well. And a lot of sheep in the back paddock.'

The dogs barked and ran out when they heard the giant tractor start up. Adam opened the door and in they jumped with wagging tails. I remembered Grandad when they all went with him throughout the day, killing any snakes which were about.

I turned to Dad. He knew I'd ask about Ted, his great Labrador.

Dad pointed. 'Up on that hill.'

I brought Martin into the conversation as well. 'Martin, do you remember when Dad sent photos of Ted? He said Ted followed me home but I heard a different story of how Dad came to have him. Ted went to live on the farm later as Dad was away a lot. He was a great mate.'

Adam joined in singing the praises of Ted the Lab. However, Dad made no further comment about how he acquired Ted.

Adam spoke. 'Well, jump in, young fella.'

Martin obeyed and off they went all day.

I heard the noise of the tractor coming back around five o'clock and saw the dogs jumping about in the cabin. My man was driving. He jumped down with a wonderful look on his face and hugged me. I brushed his shoulder and stared at him. He had a look which I had not seen before.

He patted the wheel of the machine. 'Thanks so much, Adam. Never been on one this big before. Hell, mate, air-conditioned cabin listening to Suzie's CDs and nursing the dogs all day.' Martin loves dogs as much as my family does. He shook Adam's hand.

Then something I had never remembered from the quiet Adam: Adam hugged him and said, 'Any time, young fella – any time.'

Later that night Martin was still in bewilderment about the high-tech machine with its computer which tells the driver when to sow, the expected profit, which ground has more moisture and so on. I went to sleep while he was telling me the whole story. But I was very happy we had come to the farm of my childhood.

Jane and my nephew Michael visited each day because they were not far away. There were a lot of family matters to catch up with. Shane is in the Army Reserve and is a military police officer. He told us that he was soon to go on a six-month tour of duty to East Timor. It was a training assist role and the money was very good, enough to pay off the mortgage. Dad cornered him later outside. I suspect he was telling him about some of the dangers in the developing country.

I never had any bad vibes about his tour and guessed he would come through OK. Martin said nothing about East Timor but I think he knew more than he was letting on.

I sat on my old bed in the house a few days before we left to visit Rosemary, our cousin in Canberra. Martin dearly wanted to see the War Memorial.

The room was deadly quiet. It was a breezy day and the windows were shut. I was thinking about Mum and how she used to read stories to me. I looked under the bed and there was the old suitcase of my school days. I opened the case and found my Beatrix Potter books. My hand brushed the cover of my favourite. I opened the book and sniffed. A familiar aroma of lavender and rose scent came into my senses. They were Joan's favourite and I clearly recall how she brushed the underside of her left wrist with the perfume throughout the day. I looked at my feet and saw my shiny black school shoes. My feet were crossed. I looked down and saw at my feet my old school lunch box and I opened it. There was an alfoil-wrapped sandwich with tuna, lettuce and an apple in the box as crisp as the day when I sat there. The alfoil was flat without any creases. Mum used to say, 'Smooth as a baby's bum.' That's what she was like. Who would take the trouble nowadays to run an iron over a piece of alfoil?

Wind came from nowhere, blowing the mobiles still fixed to the ceiling. I looked into the bedside dresser and froze at the sight: she was sitting alongside of me, misty, but it was her all right. I felt no freezing cold (which is supposed to be the announcement of spirits about). She was knitting and occasionally looking up. I dared not turn around lest she fade.

I picked up the Beatrix Potter book, still open at the first page, and placed it on my right side, where she sat. I whispered, 'Read me a story, Mum, please, please,' as if I had reverted to a six-year-old child.

I heard the pages being flicked over.

Then her voice, a bit quieter than I remembered, not like her great belly-rocking laugh: 'This is a good one, dear.'

I sat stunned while she read the three pages. I could not resist it. I turned my head very slowly and then she misted away to wherever spirits go when they're tired. I looked back in the mirror. She had definitely gone. I cried and cried yet felt a strong hand on my shoulder and saw her wedding ring still in place.

'Don't worry, dear. It's all in God's hands.' It was a raspy whisper.

I stood and heard a fading belly laugh which stopped near a door which I had closed but was now wide open. The wind gusted in and blew away my mum, back into the other world.

In spite of what Martin said, I hadn't gone to sleep. 'It wasn't a dream, mate.'

He knew not to meddle with my psychic senses.

I told Dad later.

'She comes to me a lot, Suzie.'

He held my hand very firmly the next day on the drive to the airport. I was in my trackies, wearing my Pumas as well.

There was a waiting time and I visited the toilet, which isn't a place one would expect to find spirits. The door was closed. I reached over for the toilet paper and was amazed when it floated in the air and then I heard her laugh, 'I'm so proud of you, love. So proud.'

I stood and flushed the loo, put the roll back on the hook and walked up to see Martin and Dad. How did I explain this one to them? I felt the flushed energy all over my face. I paused, waiting for their attention.

'Listen, both of you. She was there in the toilet. She touched me. I know it.'

Dad spoke first. 'Well, why not? Humans spend a lot of time in dunnies, you know.'

Martin giggled but stopped when Dad went on, 'Shit, she's just laughed in my left ear. It's her. I know that laugh real well.'

I hugged Dad and walked to the plane. When I looked back to wave, he was standing there having a bellowing laugh along with Mum, I opined, on his own. I guess people walking past him would cast furtive glances and rush away from the mental man talking and laughing to himself. However, I know and he knows and maybe Martin does as well, Dad was not alone, in spite of a crowded airport with strangers flashing past intent on their own journey and not noticing the man talking to a loved one in another world.

9

Suzie

Canberra

Martin handed me the typed transcript of his father's tape. Close to the end of his life, he recorded those last evocative moments alone in the cave, stuck fast after the fall of a huge boulder. It interested me more than *New Idea* with missing pages or an old *National Geographic*. I realised how eloquent his father was within a few sentences, his desperation splashed across the words.

> The stars were twinkling on the night I left Bea and my two kids. I waited like a snake on a rock for the moment when the contract of marriage, in my mind, was overdue for breaking. I am aware of what folk would say about my abandonment. Shock and unfounded assumptions. Yet I never took a glance back, which was caused by my selfish form of justification, which had been tied up in some dark cave within my shadow. The boredom of it all drove me. It was uppermost and finally arose like Neptune, with my steps hurrying away for ever. I made my gallop then just like a hyena, skulking away, tail down and fleet of foot. Here I am now, watching the glittering stars and gazing at the huge boulder perched high above and waiting, slowly inching forward to its release and another home at the foot of the cave, with a silly human squashed under it. I wish that boulder could talk. What ageless stories it's seen, mine being one of them soon.
>
> It's the third night since my sure foot gave out, and the pain comes in waves with a blue black cloud enveloping me. Maybe that's the colour of my skin which I see. My time is near and the jig is up. The easy escapes I employed for years have run out of petrol. I'm twixt and between whether I ought to end my life now. Maybe the many spider bites will have mercy on me. Maybe I'll have a stroke and then a coma. I feel God near me, I think.

I made life happen rather than let it happen and that's the rub. I used a fashion in life to dart between major and minor events, never hoping for a slack time in between. The slack times were my desert and I saw those times as rubbish accumulating, waiting for an empty status. Maybe my life was built with flaws like a house badly built with bits and pieces stuck together uncoordinated on improper foundations. Like Joseph's coat without a lining.

Marriage and kids came quickly after my discharge and a good job was there waiting. So what was wrong? Nothing. My great meals were always on time. My clothes were immaculate and then we would cuddle up after, like two spoons nestled in a cutlery drawer. Good music reigned in the house and we had top kids, who were a pride. Kids to die for.

The bridges were burnt. Maybe I thought I wasn't good enough to deserve such contentment. Perhaps I'm just an impersonator who like an actor delivers lines yet has no emotion afterwards.

What I ought to have done was constantly decipher bad messages coming in and each day make a prayer to God of gratitude. But I chose unguarded information to wreck my life and yours, dear Bea. And Jane and Martin, I was never a ladies' man and quick lust was not on the horizon, so there was no other third person in my life. I think I chose the certainty of misery rather than the uncertainty of life. The tape is running down now. Forgive me, my dears. I always loved you. I hear the boulder dislodging and I'm chucking the tape aside lest it gets squashed.

I was moved by his similes and his confessions. 'How sad, how sad,' I said. 'But Bea endured and you must be happy about the closure.'

'We are, love. It lifted her spirits from that day on. And I was at last able to get rid of the burden of not forgiving. I forgave him.'

The plane circled around Canberra and I spoke a few words to Martin after he had just woken up from a doze. 'Rosemary's part Aboriginal. Her mother Lill was the first woman of her race to make it into the Queensland police. She was married to Dennis, a detective there who investigated when Lill was raped by a sailor on leave. She refused to have an abortion and raised Rosemary on her own until Dennis, Dad's second cousin, and Lill were married. Lill was killed by a drunken driver when she was walking across the road. Rosemary's IQ was so high she was accepted for a science scholarship but as soon as she could she joined the Australian Federal Police. She served in a lot of spots until Afghanistan. I'll let her tell you her story, the bones of which you already know.'

Martin put both hands behind his head and drawled, 'Hell, what a drama. But our family are survivors as well as yours.'

We walked from the tarmac chatting all the way in to the terminal. I pointed to Rosemary in the distance. There she was with her walking stick yet still bright-eyed.

Her husband was on a job, she said when she greeted us. She had seen a photo of Martin and remarked, 'Not unlike Smithy in a way, Suzie. Maybe a bit heavier.'

She drove the short distance to her house near Lake George, the mystical disappearing lake which, I read in a glossy brochure, Aboriginals think is taboo. I was curious if that was true.

'Doesn't worry us,' she said. 'Besides, we're from another tribe.'

'What tribe?' I enquired. I ought to have remembered her humour.

'White tribe, mate.'

Martin burst out laughing but I was embarrassed.

She dug me in the ribs and said, 'Hey, I'm not going to eat you but some of my tribe did, I think, many moons ago, Lone Ranger.' Then she added, to keep the joke going, 'Hey, do you like koala on a barbecue?'

I wasn't going to answer for fear of another line but Martin did.

'What's it like?'

I waited apprehensively for her to answer.

'A bit like platypus actually.'

And then we all laughed so much that the car swerved. I was unsure if Martin knew what a platypus was but I didn't ask.

Westie came home armed with bottles of wine. He was a happy guy and warmed any room he walked into, as I soon found out. There was a lot of laughter at the barbecue, but no koalas. There was a lot of booze and we fell into bed in a drunken stupor, waking up with sore heads.

We hired a car for the day trips we'd planned and took Rosemary with us. She showed us all the sights except the War Memorial, which was earmarked for Martin the next day. I'd seen it many times.

'How did it go, Martin?'

'Great, Suzie. I saw all I wanted to see. It's really amazing. I bumped into some American tourists wearing Vietnam baseball hats and chewed the fat with them. They were armoured corps people in there in 1971. I met a military cop who was there right up till the time the NVA broke through. He was suffering really bad about the Vietnamese families and soldiers who were left behind to face the music. I wasn't aware but up to 300,000 of the South sympathisers were murdered after the hostilities ceased.'

I didn't interject while he was on a roll.

'A bloody tragedy, really. The war ended in disgrace.'

It was the only time I ever heard Martin speak out openly about the war and its consequences. He was lost a bit for a few days until we cheered him up with a visit to a military club. He played his harmonica, which revived his spirits, and no mention was made of who I was, for which I was grateful.

The rest of the time was just a quiet interlude with the reading of many emails and great booze consumed to bursting stomachs and lots of belches. Oh, and squeaky silent farts.

Rosemary was urged by Martin to tell her story and the dramas which followed. She looked at Westie, who was very lively and in an inquisitive mood and sucked the best out of Martin and me from his 1968 year in Da Nang and the Silver Star which came after, like a cart catching up to a horse.

'OK, Martin, but I'm interested in what your injury was.'

Martin looked at me. I nodded.

'Got my balls blown off, or rather 1.5 of them to be exact.'

I could see Westie cross his legs and squirm, the natural reaction from a male.

Rosemary chipped in with a cliché. 'Any change of voice?'

Martin was in on the old joke about squeaky voices and lowered his voice. 'No, ma'am, but the Bee Gees once asked me to join the band.'

Rosemary kept it going. 'I can't hear you, Lone Ranger.' And she went on, 'Any other problems, sergeant major?'

Martin replied as I knew he would, 'Not really. One consolation is I can cross my legs without an accident,' which brought the topic to a close. 'So what about you, Rosemary?' Martin leaned towards her.

It was her turn to talk about war wounds. 'OK, Martin. Let me shuffle through some papers first. Settle down and pour us all some drinks. Glasses are up there.' She pointed to the cabinet and the medal for valour was uncovered, having been gathering dust behind the glasses.

Martin picked it up. 'This is great, Rosemary. You should both be proud.'

'I suppose so. Don't want to sound ungracious. There was a big parade. I was in a wheelchair. I was thinking that my big chance to have a child was gone when my reverie was interrupted as they called my name. I felt like my hero Cathy Freeman when she once said in her great ocker voice, "I don't want a medal. I want a baby." I walked out into a life of art, like basket weaving for a while, splashing paint about and sculpture, which is my great love now. I settled into a life of invalid pensioner till something else happened.' She paused.

'What was it?' enquired my southern boy.

'I was at home here when I saw Westie hovering outside my front window. He was with me when we found the baby. He bloody near bowled me over with what he said.'

She went on after swallowing a great glass of white wine and smacking her lips. '"Rosie," he said, "I want to ghost write your story. I'll make you famous." I shook my head but he still prattled on like a woodpecker. "Imagine your story, Rosemary. What a lift to your race." He then spins it out with me being a credit to Oz. Then he blurts it out: "I love you. Will you marry me?" "What the fuck for?" I say. He's stuck for words but I take it up anyway. "So do you want to be with a celebrity and a black one at that?" "Stuff your colour," he said. "In fact, I'm darker than you once I've been out in the sun." I laugh at that and tell him to call back in a week. He does and I walk to the door naked, hoping it's him. He gulps and I watch his Adam's apple bobbing up and down. I grab him by the arm and haul him in and I says, "Slip into something more comfortable and afterwards I'll give you my answer." There he is lying on the bed in the longest pair of undies I have ever seen. They were like my grandmother's bloomers. I yank 'em off and jump on top of him.'

'What happened then?' said Martin, who was nearly crying with laughter.

'I married the little prick.'

They were holding hands at that point. Then she found the papers and the newspaper articles. We watched as she shuffled through the medical reports and the sad news that her child-rearing days were over, until she found the statement she had made at the time to the team of investigators.

'I'm sick of the sound of my voice. Have a read of this. It is of course in the first person as you'd expect.' She plonked the affidavit in front of us.

Statement of Rosemary Pearce, 25 years, AFP officer stationed at forward base Kabul, Afghanistan, obtained by Detective Senior Constable Ronald James AFP

I was on duty outside of Kabul in June 2006 in a convoy of military vehicles and in company with Shane Wallace, also a member of the AFP. I yelled out to the driver, 'Stop, stop.' I saw a small baby on the road. I jumped out to pick him up and saw something metallic inside his nappy. It was an M26 hand grenade with the pin just tied with fine cotton. I called out after I held the grenade and Shane took the baby. The pin lever was held down tightly with my right hand but I had no idea if precious seconds had been used up on the fuse. I called for all of the vehicles to form a semicircle and asked people to stay a good distance away. They obeyed and I walked slowly to the high point of the circle and hurled the grenade over the vehicles and ducked down. A huge bang was heard as the bomb exploded in mid-air. The shock wave threw me to the ground. I was in blackness. I floated out of that, I know. Yet I felt no pain and looked down. I saw I was on my back on the road and bleeding. I saw pins of light.

I woke up in hospital with machines attached and the doctor told me my shoulder and leg injuries were bad.

(Signed) R. Pearce.

'What did they say about the out-of-body episode?' Martin enquired.

'They tried to delete it but it's what I saw. They tried again and I told them to fuck off. Which they did.'

Our time had come to fly back to Western Australia and make some final farewells. We waved goodbye to Rosemary and Westie and watched as they stood in the rain on a cold frosty morning in Canberra. We'll sure miss her.

10

Suzie

Perth

Just before the plane landed, I asked Martin if he was sick of meeting relatives because there were many lined up to see both of us. For some it was a quick hello and goodbye but I had my mum's side of the family to consider, if only for a brief stop.

'You ought to know me by now, love. I am family. You've met lots of my family on our brief tours down south but they're now fans and appreciate the gifts which we've sent to the numerous children. Can't meet them all. Not possible, love. But sure, let's meet as many as we can on this last leg of the journey.'

I gave Martin a quick summary of the West side of the family. 'Joyce had an uncle who was obsessed with poo and its connection to good. My grandparents Noel and Elsie – they had a big farm as well – are dead now. Mum's funeral tore them to pieces and of course there was the young brother killed in Vietnam. The other brother fled away to the south of France somewhere. Elsie's cousin Joyce was a real card. Alternative for the times, with a bawdy sense of humour. I well remember Elsie telling me some stories about her. The last one'll show you what a different person she was. Want to hear it, Martin?'

'Yep. Go ahead.'

'A family of Aboriginal people lived a few streets away and Joyce used to speak to them, which in the racist Australia of those days was a first. The two kids of that family were good athletes and bright kids. Joyce knitted twenty-one jumpers for the local football team and the two kids were the first to receive them. From then on, once a week she would visit them and share a pot of tea on the front veranda. Joyce would have them in fits with her acid humour mocking the pompous white folk strolling past not daring to look at the black faces. Joyce would home in on any little feature like a pimple on a nose or her favourite face, which she likened to a hat full of arseholes. They grew to love her and the fresh-baked bread she gave them, along with her pickles and preserves. She taught Dorry the mother how to cook a lot more.

'Joyce understood their dreamtime long before it became politically correct. Some might say she was a bit patronising but those folk loved her for her spirit and her generosity.

'Easter time was important in her calendar and she involved her indigenous friends in one lot. It all went wrong but it started out well as a re-enactment of the last supper. A large table was in place with white ironed tablecloths. Twelve chairs were provided at the head of the table which was to face an audience of onlookers. The gramophone was set up to play religious music but unknown to her, Uncle Ron her brother, a survivor of Gallipoli, had switched the records to "The old grey mare she ain't what she used be".

'Uncle Bill, her husband, was burnt in a factory accident and could only wear a caftan. He got to be a cross-dresser and Joyce always moaned about him stealing her underwear, which felt good against his burnt skin. He was in the front row with his socks pulled right up to hide his wobbly knees. He also had a sock fetish.

'Ted, the strange one in the family – no one knew how he got there or what he did, he just moved in and was accepted, sort of like a lounge lizard – he wore pancake make-up with poorly applied bright red lipstick. They were both a sight. And they were pissed before the solemn event started.

'Their dogs and the neighbours' dogs smelt the food on display and were jumping up trying to pinch some of the fish tails. Only three disciples turned up – Joyce couldn't muster any more volunteers, because of the snobbery to which she was exposed. The small group heard the sounds of message sticks and Aboriginal men turned up. They filled the seats of the absent disciples.

'Joyce made a grand entrance dressed in a nun's outfit, supposedly Mary Magdalene. She tried to bring back some order with a narrative and urged one of her coached black kids to recite his lines. He stumbled and said, "On this night before the chooks speak, one of you will be betray me." The Aboriginal men started to eat the food and drink wine in large gulps.

'It was too much for the older drunken relative named Dollie, now very sloshed, and she shrieked with her drunken devil's laughter. The oldest black man looked at Bill and Ted and yelled, 'Bloody ugly-looking sheilas, mate,' and while all of this chaos descended, Uncle Ron had put the substitute record on full blast.

'The dogs jumped on the table and started polishing off the grub. Joyce whisked away the other wine jugs as it was forbidden then for black folk to drink. It fell silent when Mary Magdalene started to weep. Her friends comforted her and did a corroboree dance with the well known jerky movement.' I took a big breath and looked at Martin and he knew there was an ending. I had him one.

'Auntie Joyce decided never ever again to have an Easter or a Christmas celebration. She prayed to God that night for her blasphemy, which she hoped would be forgiven. So, Martin, what do you think about that?' I asked him.

He was still shaking his head and not speaking so I had to put in my dollar's worth before he did. 'Are we mad or not?'

He kept a straight face in spite of the memory of the recital. 'I believe she was far ahead of her times.'

'The sad fact, Martin, is she thought it wasn't funny.' I could see him preparing another reply.

'I think you ought to sent it to John Cleese or some of that Monty Python cast.'

'Nowadays, mate, some wit would say, "Well, that went well." What do you reckon, Martin?'

He replied by rolling his eyes, with a tonsil tone, after swallowing a peanut.

We were in Perth to catch up with relatives (what's left of them) but most of them were on holidays so it was a quick trip in a tour bus to catch some sights of Perth and then back home.

We booked a taxi to take us to the terminal. The cab driver was a chatty man and thankfully he did not recognise me in my wig and great sunglasses. But on the way, the back of my head was itchy. Something's up, I thought.

'Have you got an enemy?' the driver said.

'No, why?' I enquired because it seemed a strange question.

'A big black four-wheel drive is following us.'

We were close to the depot and stopped. The driver was paid and we jumped out almost into the arms of a TV journalist thrusting a microphone in my face. This isn't just fan stuff, I thought, and it wasn't: they were about to hound Martin.

A man wearing a dark suit stood alongside and produced an ID card which read 'PI'. 'Are you Martin MacRae?'

Martin nodded.

The PI thrust an official-looking document into Martin's hands and hopped away. I guessed he'd brought the media scrum along with him. I read the documents, which said that an Yvonne Streeter claimed that Martin was the father of her daughter – a love child from an encounter of quick lust in Sydney when Martin was supposed to be there on R&R leave in 1968. It was crap on two counts. Martin was in hospital in Vietnam and of course his medical injuries precluded any chance of fatherhood. But we didn't say anything at that time. No point raking over coals until we had a proper chance away from the tabloids.

Nevertheless, they had a field day with screaming headlines about love children, and me of course. Martin was hung out to dry, convicted in their eyes and probably in the minds of those who read the gossip columns here and in the USA, where it hit in a flash.

The same journo with her crew were camped outside overnight. We just retreated and ignored the door bell until a friendly motel manager dressed us in his mother's clothes. We fled, jumping over the back fence. Martin fell off the high heels. It was so ridiculous that I had to laugh as I tried to free his foot from a pothole. Bad idea, because a second camera crew came around the corner and filmed us dashing back inside again. The headlines the next day screamed, 'Suzie and Martin are cross-dressers'.

Apart from getting a helicopter to rescue us, all we could do was wait for our lawyer, who was faxing the USA for medical records and hospital dates. We watched our crazy Keystone Kops moments on the TV, with the manager and staff all guffawing at how stupid we looked.

Later on we walked around the streets and encountered fans who didn't hold back. One bailed us up and said, 'Don't worry. My grandfather's a cross-dresser and I have a creepy uncle who's produced three love children.'

It finally came to an end once our lawyer served a summons on the original TV station with attachments of the faxes and the disclosures. Our lawyer came with us to a rival TV station, where our innocence was spelt out. Martin didn't hold back his dry humour and had the TV reporter cackling.

She asked if he was there in Sydney on that day in 1968.

'In hospital with a wound. Back in 'Nam. There for a few months.' He showed her the date, which was held up for the viewers.

'I believe you received a Silver Star after the battle?'

Again he just smiled in answer and produced it and held it up.

'You're a staffer at the White House?'

'Yes.' Martin knew he was on safe ground.

'Suzie Smith, the famous Australian country and western star, is your wife?'

He smiled again and held up his ring finger with the USMC on top for the eyes of the viewers.

'What about the cross-dressing episode?'

He explained at length how the kind manager dressed us at the motel so we could escape and asked her if she saw it on the telly.

'Yes, with the high heels caught as well,' she said and then she started to smile as well.

'We laughed like crazy with the manager when we saw it. Bloody high heels. How do you walk in them?'

'Carefully' was her reply and she moved on. 'What was your wound. In Da Nang in '68?'

'1.5 balls blown off.'

She kept her composure, which was clever, but I could see she was starting to crack up.

'You're not able to father a child then?' Which was more of a comment than a question.

'You got it right.' He produced the copy of the medical report and showed it to the viewers.

She paused. 'What are you going to do about the scurrilous TV channel and papers who had you convicted before you could explain?'

'I could go for money but I've decided to demand a spoken and written apology from the reporter and the channel's parent companies wherever they are.' Martin was still enjoying the show.

'Has the injury caused any other problems?'

I thought that was a bit indelicate but I knew what he'd say.

He produced his best good old boy accent. 'Yes, ma'am, it has. Only when I cross my legs too quickly.'

It was too much for her and she dropped her steely-eyed look and burst out laughing. As did the audience and, from what I heard, so did the population of Australia.

Apologies thundered in one after the other. The journo was sacked. However, I think it damaged us. Some people not reading any further would have had Martin tried and convicted. It did make a difference to Martin. Part of his mojo was gone forever. He was in turmoil some nights trying to figure out how he had been named or who named him and of course why. I had no idea back then but I did know something:

my itching head after the RSL show in Australia with the woman standing with her daughter told me then about trouble looming with Yvonne Streeter. That much we knew.

Martin phoned the White House as soon as the apologies arrived and we faxed some of them as well. He was assured by his boss (and the president) that his job was safe.

'Got any idea who the man was that gave your name?'

Martin had some sleepless nights about how to answer that question. 'Not a bloody clue, Sam. Guess I might find out one day.'

The conversation petered out.

'How is Suzie?'

'Great,' he replied.

'Oh, the first lady has a pair of size ten shoes with high heels when you get back. What a bloody buzz. I could hear her and the chief laughing right across the White House. It was after the apologies came in of course. No one knew where it was going. And neither did we.'

We boarded a plane back to the USA and I realised how much Australia had changed since I left. Apart from seeing Shane and his family, I wasn't keen to travel there again.

11

Federal Prison, Washington DC

2017

From a high point in the communications control room, James and Thomas watched the cell with their revolving cameras at certain times. Victor Byron Marshall was due for release in 2018 and had given no trouble in his long haul since 2009. His brother Mark was slotted in there six years later and occupied the adjoining cell. They were left, as much as the guards could let them, to their own devices.

Tonight was the night, however, a night for James and Thomas to watch a bizarre live session which provided a fair bit of amusement to the two honest guards who would never think they were voyeurs.

'Now watch, Thomas.'

James zoomed the camera onto Victor Marshall, who was stripped naked. He lay on the top of his companion, stroking the red hair, nibbling at the ear and sliding his fingers gently on the neck, the breasts and the rib cage.

'Good foreplay, James.'

'Shush' was the reply. 'The major event's about to start.'

Victor arched his back and thrust his pelvis up and down for a few minutes and then sagged. He looked up and waved at the camera and stood up. Victor bent down and released the deflate button and watched it descend with the lookalike of his mother with the red wig flattening out. Just before it was completely flat, he jumped on the toy, grabbed the neck and squeezed out the rest of the air. The guards knew what he was doing. They were witnessing a strangulation. He stowed the sex toy under his bunk and dressed.

'And they're going to let this nut case out soon, James.' Thomas shook his head and thought, I don't think I want to watch any more now that he knows. It's only encouraging him, I reckon. And the camera was switched off.

Victor banged on his brother's cell door.

'OK, Bro' was the tired response.

'Grub's up. Come on, get up, up, up,' and Mark did because he always obeyed his brother, even when Victor sat alongside the mysterious Bill, a former bomb explosive man in the army.

'So, Bill, you can make one for me next year when I'm out?'

Mark was sick of the queries.

'So, Mark, let's go over the instructions again with Bill and me. We both have to get it right.'

Weeks of practice had honed Victor's fingers into careful manipulation of wires. Mark was there all the way.

'Bro, if it goes wrong and I die, remember I've got the big C. You've got to keep it on the boil till you're out. 2025, isn't it?'

Mark nodded sleepily. He was tired due to his constant masturbation at night and furtive smoking which his brother did not approve of.

'Stay alert, Mark. My enemies have to die. Now tell me the address once again. What are their names? Come on, tell me –get with it and stop that bloody smoking. I won't tell you again. Nicotine is disgusting.'

'Martin MacRae and Suzie Smith. OK OK OK.' It was getting monotonous, he thought.

'Good, Bro. Do you want to borrow her tonight?'

Mark shook his head. 'She smiles like Mum, Victor.'

Victor belted Mark across the back of his head, just like Gibbs in *NCIS*, which they were allowed to watch. He shouted at his young brother again. 'And stop wanking, Mark. It'll make you blind.'

Victor loved his great dream that night and remembered he was laughing. Laughing about the headlines and the telly when Martin and Suzie were dragged through the press a while back. It was so funny. He was in a good mood when he woke in the night. He reached under the bed and started to blow up the lookalike of his mother who didn't die in the night like she ought to have, he always thought, and let her mongrel husband get away with his bashings.

12

2018

Martin heard a noise outside in the driveway where he had parked his car the night before, behind Suzie's. He switched on the outside light and looked for a moment but saw nothing. He was sleepy and returned to the bed, snuggling into the fine back of his wife.

A huge noise which shook the entire spacious three-bedroom flat caused a photo of his mother and his sister to fall shattering on the floor. Martin smelt smoke and burning petrol. He ran to the front door and watched while the giant flames engulfed his car.

Suzie stood alongside holding him, in her dressing gown. 'I never saw this coming, love. Did you?'

Martin was too preoccupied with the police to give her an answer. A roasted figure of a man sat in the front seat and appeared to be dead. The sirens were coming up fast getting louder and louder. Firemen sprang from their truck dousing foam all over the burning vehicle which still smouldered. Two city detectives walked carefully up the driveway watching their footwork, not wishing to destroy any evidence. The introduced themselves. A CSI vehicle prowled into the driveway.

The next two days were a blur of paper signing and insurance stuff because part of the flat had been burnt.

Two days later

Martin and Suzie went to the CSI office in response to a phone call. The two detectives were there with beaming faces and immediately opened up the dialogue.

'Do you know this guy, Martin? Was he in the marines in '68?'

Martin stared for a second. The motive gradually dawned on him as the recognition came into his mind.

'I do, I do. It's Victor Marshall. Went down in 2009 for a lot of stuff. A drug dealer bad cop.'

'We've ID'd him from dental stuff. Have you got a clue why he would want to kill you both?'

Martin's mind went back to '68 and the gossip about Marshall. 'I need to to think about it.'

'Well, he certainly stuffed it up. Crossed the wrong wires, so the bomb people say. Do you think it was meant for your wife? 'Cos from the old file she dobbed him in for bashing her friend Joan Oliver.'

Suzie interjected. 'He did threaten us three when he was sentenced in court. Quite an outburst really.'

Martin spoke out and asked them to be patient while he recalled 1968. 'Possible, but I reckon it goes back to our marine days. I can't think what but I will try.'

They called into the Two Dogs bar and had a few drinks with the many staffers gathered there who were also shocked at the gravity of the act.

Martin sat up at four a.m. feeling that something or other had spoken to him. Suzie was on her computer typing away to Rosemary in Canberra and then to her dad, who was unwell again.

'I think I've got it, love.'

Suzie swung round after saving her text.

'Before I was shot, it actually went well till we were ordered up for the attack. Victor was trembling. He always did. He was very scared from the time we landed. He feigned sickness when his time for night patrol came up and all of us were sick of him. I called in to see him later in hospital but I was called out for another patrol and that's when I copped it. I heard Victor got a bullet wound – only a crease on the head. The guys reckoned it was self-inflicted.'

Suzie waited for Martin to speak again. She knew that he had found the truth.

He agreed. 'Bloody hell, all those years. If he'd told someone, they would've shoved him back into some paperwork job.'

'Maybe his ego couldn't stand the thought. He bragged a lot when he was with Joan. Showed us his Purple Heart as well.'

Martin swung round with anger welling up in his face. 'You didn't tell me that, Suzie.'

Suzie saw that he was owed an explanation. 'It wasn't of any consequence to me. He didn't mention you so I didn't mention him. Look, Martin, it's all over. That's the end of it.'

Which they both believed.

Bill the bomb maker sat in his cell and could hardly suppress his laughter when he heard about the explosion which all went wrong and blew Victor Byron Marshall, instead of the intended victims, Martin MacRae and Suzie Marshall, into little burnt bits. Bill sat musing on how Victor thought he could have it all. The drug ring inside and outside the prison. He imagined the thoughts of the bomber when he pushed the wrong wires together. The gleaming red eyes and the broken teeth. He thought he could go round as a cop standing over people and bashing women, women who were sick or without support. There had been a succession of them to judge from the way he used to brag. And he also bragged that he'd drowned his father and his two dogs. Bill didn't much care for fathers but he did for dogs. Dogs loved him and he loved his sister dearly. His beloved older sister. The great musician in Suzie's band. The great writer who sang like Joan Baez. The great sister who had signed over one of her houses for her younger brother when he got out of gaol. The great lady who had been bashed senseless by Victor. The great lady who died of breast cancer and maybe of the stress caused by the mongrel Victor.

'Rest in peace, Joan. And you, Victor: rest in pieces, as we used to say in the engineers till I was caught peddling the weed. I promise, dear Joan, to go straight from now on.'

13

Suzie

2024

I woke from my long sleep and looked at my bedside clock and realised I'd slept for twelve hours. The dream needed to be analysed but that was for later.

Now it was the other ritual, which was the church, and a prayer and maybe a talk with Martin's spirit. Not that he had much to say. It was just a smile, a nod and whispers which I could not decipher. The ritual was a comfort after his massive brain tumour took hold with the sudden vomits. The anger. The sparks appearing in the corner of his eyes. The loss of his freedom with the car licence and worst of all the motorised chair which propelled him around for a while. Was it all the high drama which finally undid the happy vigorous man? However, the priest had no answer.

The usual military funeral on a cold bleak December day just before Christmas 2022 and just past his Capricorn birthday. They fired the customary shots, said many words, gave me a flag and we watched when what was left of his mortal remains sank in the earth.

The end of his seventy-two-year reign. I thought my grieving was almost gone because I had mourned, was bitter, was in denial, ranting, raving, kicking chairs about when he was sitting with the morphine pump on his chest. He wished to die in the last stages and I agreed with him. If there had been a firearm in the house he would have taken his head off.

Once the ritual was done, I made my way to the Two Dogs bar and had a few beers with friends, who all said how much they missed him and what a shame it was, and (in the next breath) asked, 'Are you still singing?' just like they were putting up a closure to their own mortality. So it goes. I stayed away for a while till they recovered from Martin's death.

Dad was ill before the tumour came on Martin and I lost him in 2020 from a sudden heart attack. It was the very last trip back to Australia for the both of us. A repeat performance with Martin two years later. And how I missed Dad and his wisdom. But he's gone and that is that, so I'm told. I must get on with my life. What's left of it.

Perhaps I was thinking about the deaths of my two men and perhaps it sparked the evocative dream which I recall so vividly I can still see the very bright colours of the spectrum. But there's more. I was like an observer just watching in my Australia. And there they were, Dave and Joan my mum, having a good old Q and A.

But they must have seen me in the dream because Joan said, 'Did you see that look, Dave? Just like yours, squinting eyes and scratching the top of her head? OK, what? She's planning something. Another cupboard somewhere to sit and talk to us.'

Then Dad spoke. 'Perhaps that's a good thing, Joan.'

'You didn't tell me the whole truth, though, Dave, from your cupboard.'

Dad spoke. 'I know, but it seemed to be the right thing to do then.'

'Got you into gaol, though, didn't it? Got you raped in gaol as well.'

'I wish you wouldn't bring that up, Joan.'

'I'll tell you what I think she's going to do. She's going to clear the pantry and sit there. Maybe writing music, I hope.'

I thought about what she said in the dream and cleared the pantry. There were smells of camphor left over from Mum and surprisingly some Metsal cream which must have travelled back from Oz when I took some of Dad's shoes. He had a small foot and his joggers fitted me.

A lectern and two stools were soon in place inside the large pantry.

My guitar and music and Martin's harmonica sat on the other stool. It occurred to me he might come back one night and play it. Well, it happened. He came back another night. It wasn't music but garlic, which he munched right through his illness. The garlic smell came into my senses when I put on Dad's shoes and started walking again. Martin was with me but I didn't look around. He was with me in the Two Dogs bar with his garlic smell about but George the barman didn't say anything. George looked at me, though, when I spoke to the open space.

'Have you seen your parents, Martin?' I smiled as well and thought that George would think I've lost it, but I knew I'd get a positive answer because that's Martin – always in the affirmative. And I listened with interest to what he said.

'Sometimes, though they're not together now, but I speak to your mum Joan at times. She's a good sort. Gives me lots of advice. Like how to watch over you.'

I turned round on the stool and I thought I'd speak to George. His eyes were stary.

'How's the wife, George?' (knowing she had cancer).

'Good days, bad days. Bad days getting to beat the good ones.' He paused and said, 'Jeez, I miss him and your songs, Suzie.' He would not have known that Martin was with me on the other bar stool.

14

Washington DC

2025

In the three-bedroom flat, the large man wearing the balaclava lay dead with his head twisted at an awkward angle. The owner of the flat, Suzie Smith, was busy at her fridge cutting up small goods and glanced furtively at the detectives.

The detectives already had a statement from the neighbour who raised the first alarm and advised them, 'Not much use trying to get anything from her. She's gone gaga.'

They realised the truth of the statement when Suzie disrobed and stood naked, urging them to sing with her the US national anthem. They looked inside the freezer and saw row upon row of frozen shoes and knew it was useless to interview her.

The ambulance came and took her away while she smiled and waved at the police officers, who gazed own at the body, a man they recognised as Mark Marshall, recently released from the federal prison. They assumed a lot and saw a lot but were stuck for a motive as the owner, obviously a martial arts expert, judging from all the belts found in the flat, had broken his neck. He had certainly been an intruder and the case was closed.

'Stiff shit for him,' said the CSI man named Johnathon.

And Stan the detective agreed, hoping, after gaping at the well built naked woman, that his erection would soon subside.

They were not aware that she had lured Marshall there with a form of entrapment after he stalked her. It was payback time after all the hurts she had suffered but first she had to put on a convincing act of having dementia. The time would come later for her to pretend to be better for release

Nine months later

Suzie was on her walk back to the flat reflecting on the demise of Mark Marshall. She spoke to a spirit who claimed to be her double. For the sake of simplicity she called the spirit Number Two. However, Suzie was not in total agreement with the advice offered by Number Two. When the intruder broke in nine months ago, however, it was the only plan available and she always had confidence in Plan A.

Suzie received some advice which she acted on regarding Mark Marshall. It was in-the-moment speech with the intruder.

'Number One calling. I hear footsteps outside.'

'Yes, Number One, this is Number Two speaking. Listen for the sound of broken glass right now.'

'Number One calling. I hear it right now. He's here.'

'Watch out, Number One. He's wearing a balaclava. Go into attack mode *now*.'

'Number One calling. What do I do again?'

'Jesus Christ, Number One, kick him in the balls. When he falls, rabbit chop his neck, OK.'

'Number One calling. It's done. What now, Number Two?'

'Break his bloody neck. You're trained do it. Now, Number One.'

'I heard the click. It's done, Number Two. What now?'

'Number One to Number Two: I run next door and go into my gaga act like we agreed. They'll call the cops. Is that right, Number Two?'

Number Two did not answer.

'Number One calling again. Yes, it's done. I hear the sirens coming, Number Two.'

'OK. Your last message was broken. When the cops come, make sure your boots are in the fridge and don't forget, Number One, to put on the tape of the national anthem and drop your robe. You're to be naked, remember, and get the cops to sing along with you. Conduct the choir with the tongs. That will nail it. You'll go to a funny farm but only for nine months. It'll all have blown over by then and you'll be able to go back home. Got that OK, Number One?'

'Yes, Number Two. Should I talk to you in the home?'

'Number Two calling. Not actually recommended, with all the trick cyclists poking and prodding. OK, Number One?'

Suzie took the advice and thought about a lot in the home until she was released.

'Number Two, this is Number One calling after a nine-month break. I have some reservations about all of this, actually. I think I'm coming unglued. What do you think, Number Two?'

'Number One, that's bullshit and you know it. Let's go home and have a drink. You're out and in the clear. Stop worrying.'

Suzie set two glasses of white wine out. Number Two's glass had not been raised.

'Number Two, please respond. You haven't drunk yours.'

There was total silence.

Suzie woke up during the night and saw that Number Two's glass was still untouched. She knew then what she had to do. She dialled the number of a therapist she knew. He was James Morris, the retired federal consultant, who was a friend of Martin.

'James, I need help,' and then, as an afterthought, she dialled Johnno's number.

Detective Stan Harris sat in the cheaper coffee shop close to the station because he was scraping every dollar together since his pretty model wife, the Golden Goddess, had left. When she was naked she stood like a marble statue, even a blue heron, while he humped away without much love. It was always the knee trembler because she hated getting her hair in a mess by lying down. He figured she was after more gold than he could supply so he let her go.

The naked figure of Suzie Smith standing there nine months ago with the dead intruder and singing the national anthem urging them to sing along and conducting with two barbecue tongs was not only funny but sexy. He felt the rising in his loins whenever he thought about her. But she'd been sent to the funny farm.

'Hey, Stan, it's me, Johnno.'

'How's the new job, Johnno?'

Johnno came over and pulled out his wallet, which bulged with money. 'Good. Lots more money. Private is the way to go.'

Stan remembered the last job at the flat before Johnno left and also the great body of the fifty-five-year-old naked Suzie once again. She was haunting his dreams.

'Hey, Stan, remember Suzie Smith who killed the intruder in her flat?'

'How could I forget? Naked and all of us singing the national anthem. In the funny farm.' Stan wondered how strange it was when he was just thinking about the gorgeous woman and his erection was still rising under the table, hopefully out of sight of nosey Johnno.

'Nup, she's out. I forgot to tell you before. She rabbit punched him. She kicked him in the nuts and the rabbit punch followed afterwards.'

Stan sat up with a question. 'So how did you catch up with her, Johnno?'

'Bloody hell, Stan, she was sitting on a stool in Two Dogs bar and I hear a voice. "Hi, Johnno," she says. "Still breaking necks, Suzie?" I says. "Only my Dad and Martin called me Suzie, God rest them," she says. "How's the dementia?" I says. "What dementia?" she says.'

Stan thought for a while and then the penny dropped. And he stroked his chin beard and started to giggle about how clever she had been. 'Well, I call that justice, mate. How often do we see that now? Christ, what a woman. So she planned it all. I remember there were reports of a man stalking her.'

'There's more. She's back on stage back on her country and western gigs. In fact, she gave me two tickets for Saturday.'

'Shit, can you get me one?'

'Piss off, Stan.'